Lili and Chiara love their jobs at *Fee Kaffee,* but after the peach schnapps and poteen incident sets off a family row, their home life feels increasingly restrictive. When Irish Toby tosses them charmed apples, they decide to make a Christmas wish. The café offers a venue, but their apples have vanished. It seems they're not the only ones using *Fee Kaffee* for a little Christmas magic.

Yannick has worked for Martina Bless for three years. He likes the job, but Martina's twin nieces constantly distract him. In an effort to get them off his mind, he makes a charmed cake meant to attract his heart's desire. He's just added two spare apples to his recipe when he hears someone in the café.

The twins need men, and Yannick needs a woman. It might be a match made in heaven, but there are two of them and only one of him. The three of them go to Yannick's house to thrash the matter out. Once they find their solution, every-thing is fine . . . maybe.

Meanwhile, at the café, Martina faces the post-Christmas rush with a staff gone suddenly AWOL. The only clue she has is a napkin with a two-word message saying *Just Eloped.*

Just Eloped
Copyright © 2020 Lark Westerly
ISBN: 978-1-4874-3100-6
Cover art by Martine Jardin

Published by eXtasy Books Inc or
Devine Destinies, an imprint of eXtasy Books Inc

Look for us online at:
www.eXtasybooks.com or www.devinedestinies.com

Just Eloped
A Fairy in the Bed

By

Lark Westerly

DEDICATION

If you love a bit of Christmas magic, this one is for you.

Author's Note

The *Fairy in the Bed* series features a sprawling cast of characters who wander in and out of one another's stories. For more about this series, visit Lark's website at https://larksinger.weebly.com

Just Eloped stands alone, but you may recognise some of the characters and settings.

Lili, Chiara and Yannick appeared in *Geese a Laying*, which tells the story of what happened to Martina while her staff went AWOL.

Martina Bless appeared in *Geese a Laying, Sunshower,* and also in the *Counterpoint* books. Dequan Qin was in *Geese a Laying* and had a small but pivotal role in *Queen of the May.* They reappear in *Arms Around Her.*

Tab and Josefa appear in several books. They met in *Sam and the Sylvan.*

Like *Geese a Laying,* and *Queen of the May, Just Eloped,* is set in 2020. When I wrote *QotM*, Covid19 wasn't even thought of. By the time it was published, we were in the middle of a pandemic. Since it was far too late to rewrite the story, I had to let it be. My philosophy is that as the world of *Fairy in the Bed* is not *quite* our world, we can accept that in that reality the pandemic didn't happen in 2020.

CHAPTER ONE: IT'S A TWIN THING

Lili Bless, Christmas Eve

Lili woke at six o'clock on Christmas Eve, just as her sister blinked awake in the second twin bed.

They sat up in unison.

Nina, their mother, didn't understand how they did that.

"It's a twin thing." That was their answer to everything.

"Don't be ridiculous. You're not even identical."

Nina had taken them for genetic testing when they were four.

Anyway, Lili had darker hair and bluer eyes.

Nina didn't believe in the *twin thing*. She didn't believe in *the sight*, either. The twins did. *Tante* Martina had it. The occasional information that came into Lili's mind might have come from *the sight*, but she thought it just as likely it came from Chiara.

They turned to their wardrobes on opposite sides of the room. Lili picked out a pair of jeans she hadn't worn in months and a pink singlet top. She conjured them on.

Behind her, Chiara closed her closet door with a bang.

She turned to face her sister across the room.

"Dammit."

"Twinned again," Chiara said mournfully. She had on an old pair of jeans and a pink singlet top as well. They weren't identical to Lili's, but they were close enough.

"I'll change. Otherwise Mum will think we did it to annoy," Lili said.

"She won't see us. We'll get coffee at the firm."

The firm was their name for *Fee Kaffee*, the café where they had worked for the past three years. It belonged to their aunt,

1

Martina Bless. Martina was unruffled, fair-minded, and sometimes formidable. She scared the pants off patrons who got out of line.

"Our Martina's better than a cattle prod to the balls when she's roused." That was what Uncle Dario said. He was only six years older than the twins and their mother disapproved of him.

Lili conjured two bananas out of the kitchen as they headed for the garage. She could have conjured coffee, but the stuff Nina bought was denatured, decaf and tasteless. They'd tried buying their own supply. Nina called that ridiculous.

Lili stuck half a banana in her mouth and chose a bike at random. They'd each bought an identifying sticker so they'd know whose bike was whose, but they had accidentally chosen the same ones.

In unison, they trod on their pedals and wheeled out of the garage and along the quiet street.

"*Zwillingsschwester?*"

"Hm?" Lili focused. Chiara only ever called her *twin sister* for something important.

"Identical twins?" Chiara suggested.

"Been there, done that, and they were —"

"Identical dicks."

"Not even pretty ones."

"Bendy and —"

"Ugh."

They canted around a corner and another. The market was two blocks ahead.

They stopped together in a spurt of gravel before they wheeled their bikes into the racks provided for the market.

Lili conjured the wide-mouthed market baskets their aunt insisted on.

"I saw that, Lili Bless!" Tab Merriweather called, grinning at them from across the parking area.

Tab had three look-alike brothers, so his habitual focus on detail meant he could easily identify the twins.

Lili gave him the finger. "Oh, go and yodel Josefa."

"Go and *what*?"

Chiara flicked a glance at Lili, and they chorused, "Stick your dick where the sun don't shine."

"Josefa *is* my sunshine." Tab's attention turned to his betrothed, who was desperately poking at the keyhole of an ancient yellow utility.

"Shit-shit-shit, it's stuck in the hole," she yelled.

The twins laughed.

"Tango and Tempo? Togetherness would be normal to them," Lili pondered *sotto voce*.

"Too young," Chiara objected.

"They're legal. Let's ask Tab."

"Ask me what, you mad *mädchens*?" Tab had unnaturally good hearing.

Lili looked him over. The Merriweather brothers were all tall with dark hair, pale skin and grey-gold eyes. Tab, the eldest, was betrothed to Josefa, and Timbre, the youngest, was in love with a courtfolk lady. That left Tango and Tempo in the middle.

Tab backed up against the ute with Josefa. "Why are you two looking predatory?"

"Would Tango and Tempo like us for Christmas, do you think? Or maybe we could have *them?*" Chiara asked.

"Not if you're going to look at them like that."

"We'd make very nice Christmas presents. So would they." Chiara sounded injured.

Tab crossed his forefingers and put up his hands. "Save me, Josefa. They're doing that x-ray spooky-eyed twin thing."

"Never mind, I'm sure you've got nice bones," Josefa said. She turned to the twins. "You can't have Tab. He's all mine. You have good taste in men, but I warn you, Tan's got that nice brae halfling — Alys something — in his sights."

"No dice then. We need a matched pair." Lili waved to Josefa and grabbed her sister's free hand. "Dylan it is."

There was only one of Dylan Castle, but that wasn't the point. He was a possible solution to their other problem which, loosely speaking, boiled down to *How to Get out of Dodge.*

Dodge was their name for their parents' house, which felt increasingly like a too-tight pair of jeans.

It was definitely too tight in the knicker department. Their unsatisfying liaison with the identical twins had taken place in the men's van after work, and the logistics, as well as the twins, had proved impossible.

They entered the market and bought tomatoes and a box of eggs from Jeremy Costas.

"Bother. We ought to have got the eggs last," Lili said.

"They're padded with feathers," Jeremy said.

"Really?"

He shrugged. "Where there's poultry, there's feathers, and they're more environmentally sound than packing peanuts."

Lili thanked him, and they moved off in concert along the front line of stalls.

"Target locked in," Chiara said presently.

Lili looked at the tall young man with the mixed vegetable stall. He had brown hair, blue eyes and a beauty spot on his cheek. She caught his eye and smiled demurely.

"Hi, Dylan."

"Hey, Lili. Hey, Chiara. What can I do you for?"

"We don't need much today, since the café's closed tomorrow for Christmas," Lili said.

"I've got some nice fresh peas and these long radishes."

"Yes, and we need some of the rocket for pizzas."

"And potatoes. We could make potato salad and take the leftovers home for supper," Chiara suggested.

Dylan said, "Those baskets must get heavy. Do you want

me to deliver them to Ms Bless after I finish up here?"

"That's sweet of you, but Yannick needs them right away," Lili said. She opened her purse, making a production of finding the right money. Stallholders got uneasy when she conjured.

"How's life in the share house? Still packed in like kippers?" she added casually.

Dylan said, "It's even more kippery now. Ty moved in last week. You know—my cousin? Better for the rent, but he's got all this *stuff.*"

"Yes, we know Ty." She put her purse away. "C'mon, Chi."

Dylan said, "There's a party at the *Apple Crate* on the twenty-seventh if you'd like to come with."

"We don't have a car," Lili said, smiling at him. He was such a nice lad—pity about the cousin, his cousin's stuff, and the kipperish state of his share house.

"We can take you. Double date."

"You and Ty?" Lili said.

"Sure."

"Catch you, maybe," Chiara said over her shoulder as she walked on.

"Hey, Lili . . ."

"Yes?"

"Um—you *are* over eighteen?"

"Coming up twenty-one," she said. "Why?"

"Just checking before I gave you this." Dylan handed her a small brown bag. "Merry Christmas."

Lili tucked it into her pocket. "Merry Christmas, Dylan."

"That's a bust," she said when she caught up with Chiara at the soft fruit stall.

"Even Dodge is better than a kipperish place with Ty in it," Chiara said. "Dylan is so sweet, but Ty—"

"You know what Uncle Dario says."

"Damp hands mean sloppy cock." Chiara paused in

5

thought and then said, "I wonder how he knows? He's not gay, is he?"

"No. Maybe bi-curious."

"Or just omnivorous. Do you think *he* might know someone with a spare room?"

Lili regretfully shook her head. "Anyone Uncle Dario knows would be in Melbourne. Besides, he'd tell Dad."

"Dad would tell Mum and then the shit would hit the fan."

"What's wrong with us . . . with Mum? We're nearly fucking twenty-one!" Lili said.

"At least we've got the firm and *Tante* Martina. Pity we can't live with her," Chiara said.

"She likes her privacy. Besides, the shit really would hit the family fan if we did that."

Chapter Two: Peach Schnapps and Poteen

Chiara Bless, Christmas Day

Chiara wanted to sleep in on Christmas Day.

That was never going to happen. Their brother, Luca, was still young enough to be excited about presents and trees.

Every year, they'd petitioned for a proper tree, but Nina preferred her table-top no-mess model with the rigid limbs.

Chiara made an effort, anyway. She talked Lili into wearing the new shirts Nina had bought them.

Lili's was silky plain green with a handkerchief hem, and Chiara's was crisp red and white, with a poinsettia splashed on the front.

They looked at themselves in the mirror with considering expressions.

"If we'd picked out one ourselves, which would it be?" Chiara wondered.

"Neither. They're awesome. Just not *us*," Lili said.

They got through the day, helped by cherries and chocolates, Christmas cake, Christmas carols and a mad game of Christmas Charades with Luca.

By ten o'clock, the twins were family-Christmassed-out and they retired to their room.

"Market tomorrow. Are we going to say yes to Dylan's party?" Chiara said.

"Not much point. But speaking of . . ." Lili produced a mini bottle of peach schnapps from her knicker drawer and poured some into their water glasses.

They sipped in unison.

It was revoltingly . . .something. Chiara said, "Where did

you get that?"

"Dylan gave it to me yesterday. Look, he's put a ribbon around the neck. *Sweet.*"

"Nice Dylan is plying you with alcohol? Why?"

Lili shrugged. "He *is* nice, and he wants to get into my pants."

"No use when he's not near your pants when you drink it."

"That's why he gave it to me yesterday in a public place. It's a blue feather present. You know, a gift like the ones gentleman bowerbirds give to lady bowerbirds. *See, I really am a handsome bird. I could give you a good time.*"

"Does he know alcohol won't affect us?"

"Doubt it. I've never disclosed to him. Have you?"

"Of course not. Why would I?"

They never disclosed what they were to humans unless asked directly. There was no need and no point. It was too much trouble and human reactions were too predictable.

Alpenfee? What's that?

Fairies from the alplands over there.

The what where?

Fairies, seriously?

Where's your wand? Do some magic for me.

Um . . . is this you telling me you like girls?

Seriously — you can't get drunk?

Well . . . that sort of depends.

Much too much trouble.

Chiara waited a beat and then said, "I've got something that *will* affect us, though."

"What? How? Where?"

Chiara opened her own knicker drawer and unearthed a tiny black bottle with an enamel shamrock on the neck. "Leprechaun poteen," she explained, conjuring out the stopper.

Lili reached for the bottle. "Now you're talking! Who gave you this? Has he got a brother?"

"It was Cèilidh from the *Pride of Erin*. Her da makes it *over there* for the pub, but of course it's not on the *general* shelf. *Can't be havin' the human patrons flat on their backs now, darlin'.*" She smiled as she mimicked their friend's soft leprechaun accent. "She gave us this as a love gift for Christmas. She said it had a little charm to cheer us up. *No harm.*"

Lili tipped half the bottle into her glass and returned the balance to Chiara, who did the same.

Chiara sipped and made a face. "That's worse, if it's possible."

"Well—can't waste it. If we pour it down the sink, it might eat through the pipes. Merry Christmas, *Zwillingsschwester!*" Lili held her nose and drained her glass.

"*Prost!*" Chiara finished hers in three desperate swallows.

They eyed one another doubtfully.

"That was—"

"Quite likely—"

"The worst—"

"Thing we ever drank."

They settled back to await results.

"Feeling cheerful yet?" Lili asked after a while. "Or is the cheerful bit just that you feel cheerful because you don't have any more of that stuff to swallow . . . uh . . . what?"

Chiara's tongue felt funny. "Whoa!" Green sparkles danced in her vision and she heard a flourish of fiddle music.

That's odd. It doesn't go with Christmas.

Her head cleared and she felt the urge to dance, so she did.

Lili must have felt the same because she got up and began something that looked like a braefolk sword dance.

"You can't do that to fiddle music," Chiara protested, between giggles.

"You can to bagpipes."

They caught arms and swung between the two beds, leaping like gazelles.

They were still dancing to their poteen-induced inner music when their door burst open.

"Whatever are you girls *doing* in here?"

Nina stood staring at them as if they'd grown antlers.

Chiara caught Lili's eye, and they doubled up in a storm of laughter. "Dancing!" they said in chorus.

That look of their mother's face was almost worth the row that followed.

CHAPTER THREE: WISHES FOR KISSES

Lili, Saint Stephen's Day

Lili was still smarting from the family row when she woke the next morning.

Their mother could be cutting when she was out of temper. She'd had a lot to say before she wound down.

The torrent of criticism seemingly had little to do with her daughters' Christmas nightcap, though it did begin with *irresponsible* for mixing drinks and for touching poteen at all.

It continued with *thoughtless* for making a rumpus and keeping their parents awake.

Then came *selfish* for setting a bad example for their brother.

This was followed by foolish, wasteful and ungrateful for not making something of their lives.

Untrustworthy and sly for sneaking poteen into my house.

Irresponsible came around again, and then *bad example,* but this time that was about their friends and their aunt, Martina, who *encouraged* them in *culturally inappropriate behaviour.*

When *wasteful and ungrateful* rolled around again, Lili was unwise enough to say it would have been wasteful to throw the poteen away.

Their father joined the fray then. Lili knew he wasn't angry about the schnapps, poteen and dancing. He was angry because their mother was angry and they all, except for Luca, had to work in the morning.

Lili dressed and tied up her hair.

"Breakfast at the firm?" she said to Chiara.

"Sure. Mum might have poisoned the bananas."

"She wouldn't do that."

"No. You're right. That was uncalled for. But a lot of what *she* said was uncalled for. What possible harm were we doing?"

"We drank charmed poteen."

"Yes, but we *knew* it was charmed. Cèilidh's a darling. She'd never do anything to hurt us — or anyone. It was just a little bit of Christmas fun for us."

They went to the market, and Lili thanked Dylan again for the gift.

"Coming to the party?" he asked.

"Is there likely to be peach schnapps involved?"

"Sure to be," he said.

Lili patted his cheek, making him blush. "I hope you have a lovely life. You deserve it," she said.

They moved on to Irish Toby's apple truck.

"Smile, darlin's."

Lili smiled at him. It was difficult not to. Irish combined working the markets with riding for local racing stables. Like many jockeys, he had a wiry body and a mobile face that could have been any age from twenty to forty. Unlike most jockeys, he probably ate whatever he wanted and never put on a superfluous gram of fat.

"That's better!" He beamed and simultaneously tossed them each an apple. *"Wish gift for a kiss, girleens!"*

"Cut the blarney, Irish." Lili kissed her fingers and flicked them in his direction. "There's your kiss. Where's my wish?"

Irish touched his cheek and winked at her. "You're holdin' it."

"The apple?"

"Be sure to share it wid the other parties, now, or else it won't work."

Irish raised his brows at Chiara, who blew him a kiss as well.

"Same deal for you, darlin'. Tis the season for Christmas

kindness."

Lili's spirits rose a notch from his *joie de vivre.*

"What is it with him and his blarney?" Chiara asked.

"Who knows. He's got the leprechaun babble down a treat, but he can't possibly be a pure leppy. His skin's too pale."

"Could be a halfling or a quarterling. Or maybe he's just a real Irishman who likes to ham it up."

"Not him. He's a fairy all right. Does anyone kiss him for real when he does that blarney routine?" Lily wondered aloud.

"Cèilidh Acushla does."

"Cèilidh kisses everyone, even us. It's nice."

"Kissing girls is nice?"

"I don't know in general. She's the only one I've ever kissed." She brooded. "Haven't kissed *anyone* in weeks, other than the duty-peckery kind of kiss."

"Maybe we need to try single dating again," Chiara said.

They exchanged glances and said, in unison, "Nah."

They conjured their baskets ahead for Yannick to unpack and then they rode on to *Fee Kaffee.*

It had just gone half-past seven. *Tante* Martina was setting up the café for opening.

"*Guten morgen, Tante,*" Lili said.

"*Kaffee?*" Chiara asked.

"*Guten tag, mädchens.*" Martina hugged them in turn. "Did you have a good Christmas?"

"Yes, except—" Chiara began.

"Our cruel aunt gave us just one day off," Lili interrupted. Martina and their mother didn't really get on, so Lili liked to keep Dodge business out of the café.

"I am a very cruel aunt," Martina agreed smugly. "Make me a coffee, yes, and take one to Yannick."

The kitchen was sweet with the aroma of baking bread and the richness of *alpenkuchen.* There was something else that Lili

13

couldn't identify.

Yum! She stole a ginger biscuit from a cascading pile. It was still warm.

She was about to take a second one when the biscuits vanished and reappeared in a lined tin.

"Yannick," she protested, identifying the culprit without difficulty.

"Grmph."

She poured the coffee and carried a cup to Yannick. He was up to his wrists in a strange dark dough that bubbled as he punched it down. "Looks scary, *kleiner Bruder*."

Yannick's dark, secretive gaze flicked in her direction.

"Smells of cherries." Lili put down the cup and dabbled her forefinger in the dough. It stuck, and she sucked it off.

"Yummm," she mumbled around her fingertip. She extended her middle finger and captured another blob of dough.

Yannick's capable hands clenched for a split second before he swept the dough into a ball and dumped it into a tub of flour.

Hands off my dough. That was the implication.

She supposed he had a point. Now it was deflated, it was a very small dough-ball.

"May I have another biscuit, then?"

"Anything for you, my lovely."

Lili's brows flew up. Forgetting the biscuit, she scooted back to the coffee and carried three cups into the café proper.

"Yannick spoke five whole words!" she announced.

Tante Martina's wide grey gaze turned on her. "Really? Did you put a compulsion on him?"

"I wouldn't do that to him."

Her aunt looked startled. "Just a joke, *meine Liebste*."

"I know. Sorry." Lili bit her lip. The row with Nina still rankled. And now her aunt's baker was being peculiar.

She drank her coffee, and then she and Chiara changed into

their dirndls.

Nina considered the wearing of dirndls an affectation. Alpenfee *mädchens* wore them as a matter of course *over there* in the alplands of the fay home realm, but the Bless family had *lived human* for over a century. Nina was a Bless-by-marriage, but *her* family, the Lucans, had *lived human* for even longer. She had little contact with them, which Lili might have thought sad if she hadn't known Nina liked it that way.

"You wear scrubs," Lili pointed out when Nina mentioned *those strip-o-gram uniforms* once too often.

"There's some point to those, Elizabeth."

Nina was a devoted and loving wife to Florien. She doted upon Luca. It was the twins she clashed with, ever since the Difference of Opinion, as Martina called it, when the twins chose employment at *Fee Kaffee* over Nina's insistence on higher education.

More than three years on, Nina still hoped her daughters would see the folly of their ways and *do something worthwhile with your lives.*

Dodge was getting beyond uncomfortable. Hence Lili's and Chiara's efforts to *Get out of Dodge*. They didn't want to abandon their family. They wanted to love them on less dutiful terms.

To Get out of Dodge, they needed a suitable place to live. They wanted suitable men. They hoped to find a suitable place and invite the suitable men to share it *ad-lib*, but the chances of getting what they wanted anytime soon seemed increasingly slim.

Lili did flowers, choosing Christmassy red and white from Martina's small garden. Chiara filled bird feeders outside the café.

At eight o'clock, Martina opened the doors, and by five past, the first patrons came in for a quick bite before post-Christmas shopping, or for take-away coffee to carry home or to work.

Nina and Florien had jobs in essential services, so they were back on call. Lili didn't expect *them* to come for coffee. Luca might come for cake, though, if his best friend's mother, who was happy to mind him along with her three sons, felt the need for something nice.

Once the doors were open, it was all go.

At nine-thirty, Yannick came silently out of the kitchen.

"*Auf Wiedersehen, kleiner Bruder.* I hope you had a good Christmas," Lili said. She usually phrased her comments like that with Yannick. That way, his habitual grumble could be taken as a response.

He glanced at her and then looked away. "*Danke, lovely. I have hopes.*"

WTF?

Emboldened, she said, "I hope you got that bubbly dough baked."

A wintery smile flickered, so brief she thought she'd imagined it.

WTF? WTF?

Lili looked to see if Chiara or Martina had noticed. When she looked back, Yannick had slipped through the connecting door to the garage where he parked his van.

Chapter Four: A Special Breed

Chiara, Saint Stephen's Day

There was something weird going on with Lili.

Chiara felt that in the strange flare of excitement she sensed in her twin.

The café was busy and none of the casual staff had come in, so it was a while before she had a chance to corner her sister.

At two-thirty the traditional lull gave them time to get on top of the washing up. Yannick had done some of it, but more had built up since he left for his break at nine-thirty.

Usually, the twins took it in turns to have breaks, but today had been busy.

Thankless slave labour was what Nina called work in the café, but *Tante* Martina paid well, and she had taught them a great deal about the management of people and business.

"I wonder where Yannick goes for his breaks," Lili said as they worked through the silverware.

"Limbo?" Chiara guessed.

"Why would you say that?" Her sister sounded sharp.

"I mean, who can say? For all we know, he lives in a cuckoo clock." She frowned. "I can't imagine him in a messy share house or in a flat, and *definitely* not in some kind of Dodge situation. Does *Tante* know his address?"

Lili shrugged.

Chiara moved to pour afternoon coffee. "*Tante*, do you know where Yannick lives?"

Martina took her cup. "Why?"

"We were just wondering. He must live somewhere, but we never see him anywhere else but here."

"Bakers are a special breed, my dear. They have to be, to survive on such unsociable hours."

Chiara considered that with a frown. She and Lili worked long hours, but they had time off when the casual staff came in, and *Tante* Martina would always let them flex their time if it was important.

Yannick started work at three in the morning, went off at nine-thirty, and returned in time to bake the scones for afternoon tea. He was sometimes still there when they departed.

That suddenly struck her as sad.

"We should get another baker," she said.

Martina gave her a strange look. "Instead of Yannick? Why? He's very good at what he does and he's utterly reliable. I'm fortunate to have him. I know he's no conversationalist, but I didn't hire him for his sparkling personality."

"I meant, as well as Yannick."

"I see. I have thought of finding a hob baker so we could serve courting cake and those cheese things they do, but even a hob might find sharing the kitchen with Yannick a bit of a strain. Don't look like that, my dear. I'm not being unkind, but *Fee Kaffee* runs as well as it does because we have such a tight crew and the dynamic *works*."

Chiara accepted that as another of *Tante* Martina's little business lessons. She'd promised their parents that the twins would be trained in all service and management aspects of the café, and she had kept her word meticulously.

"Dynamics have to *work* in life," Martina said, almost to herself. "That's why so many businesses and relationships fail. People have their own ideas. They *assume,* and they expect other people to match up to their assumptions. Mostly, they don't. At *Fee Kaffee,* we all know what to expect of one another. We *assume* each of us will play a certain role, but we can do that because experience has proved it's safe to do so."

Chiara returned to the kitchen and glanced at Lili. Usually, she knew what her twin was thinking without conscious effort. Today, Lili's edges were sharp. Maybe the row with Nina was still hurting her.

"We've got to fix our dynamic and get out of Dodge," she said.

"We've been trying to do that for weeks," Lili reminded.

Chiara gripped her sister's hand. "We've *assumed* we have to do things the way other people do them. You know . . . go to parties and trawl for share houses with spare space at a reasonable rent."

"So?"

"We're not like other people. We have the twin thing."

"Are you suggesting we need to try and . . . what did Mum call it . . . Decouple? We had enough of that when she pushed us into different electives in school."

"I don't think we should try to decouple. I think we should embrace what we are. *All* that we are. We're twins and we're alpenfee fairies. Remember Irish Toby? He's definitely embracing what he is—whatever that is."

Lili said, "There's only one of him, and besides, he's a bit liberal with the kisses. He asks everyone female, I think, on the grounds that he'll strike lucky sometimes. I don't know what good blown kisses are to him, but I expect he has an over-active cock."

Chiara laughed. "I wasn't thinking of his cock, Lil. I'm sure it's charming, but probably a bit green if he really is a leppy. I was thinking about his Christmas wish apples."

Holding hands, they stared at one another.

"Making a wish is a bit . . . well . . ."

"Mum would absolutely *not* approve. Neither would Dad, really."

"Uncle Dario would say *go for it, twinnies*."

"Uncle Dario is an egger-onner. You know why most people don't go the wish route to fix their lives?"

"Because most people don't believe in wishes?" Lili suggested.

"No, *Dummkopf*. It's because it's so chancy. It depends on the right fairy being there at the right time to service the wish . . . and the ethics have to work out."

"Oh, I see! We *are* the right fairies and our ethics are fine," Lili said.

"So —"

"We can totally service a wish for one another!"

They loosed hands and pointed to one another.

"Right fairy. Right ethics," they said together.

"Now, we just need the right time."

"Wishes can go horribly wrong," Chiara said.

"*Life* can go horribly wrong, *Zwillingsschwester*. If we stay in Dodge much longer, we'll either knuckle under or else we, or Mum, will say something that we won't be able to come back from."

They eyed one another doubtfully.

"Are we going to do this?"

"It's still the Christmas season, but not for long. Let's get out of Dodge," Lili said.

A slight change in air pressure informed them the garage door had opened. Yannick was back from his break.

He stepped into the kitchen in a waft of warm baking spice and vanished into the larder to measure flour and buttermilk for the café's famous high-top scones.

When Chiara peeped in, he was rolling out the dough on a marble slab. "Yannick?"

He glanced up.

Faced with his unreadable gaze and improbably dark eyes, Chiara backed away. Lili must have been imagining things.

Not even a grumble.

She went out to help Martina set up the cups for afternoon tea.

Chapter Five: Langel Liebeskuchen

Yannick Langel, Saint Stephen's Day

At six o'clock on Saint Stephen's Day, Yannick Langel was simmering a fruit decoction. It was risky to begin so early in the evening, but it had to be finished while the cake was still warm.

He'd got the basic recipe as accurate as he could. He had put his own stamp on the baking. This was *his* wish and it had to be tailored to *him*.

He heard the three Bless ladies out in the café. What were they doing out there? It was well past closing time, and they should have all gone home.

He liked Mistress Martina. She'd hired him without fussing about paperwork.

He remembered how she'd smiled when he gave his date of birth and said cheerfully, "*Gott im Himmel!* You'll fit right in with the girls."

He hadn't asked for clarification, but she'd explained anyway.

"My nieces are twins. Lili was born at five minutes to midnight. Chiara followed ten minutes later, so they are technically a day apart. You, my lad, fall on the very next day after Chiara."

The nieces were fresh-faced younger versions of Mistress Martina. Having the two of them around him was disturbing. He thought he could have dealt with one. Two were difficult. He could be aware of one and carefully distance himself from her fizzing personality. Suddenly, the other would impinge on his vision. One might distract him with her apple-and-cherry scent while the other whipped away a too-warm cake for cutting. One might open the oven at an inopportune time, and the other might suddenly pop into the larder and peer at something he was mixing. She might even ask him how he was making the mixture do *that*. He never answered because, of course, he didn't know. He was a Langel, and baking was in his blood.

The twins had learned better eventually, and now, after more than three years, they treated his creations with more respect, and they'd stopped pestering him for responses.

They talked together in odd, disconnected sentences, and sometimes in one long sentence with each of them contributing. They held hands, sometimes. They caught emotions and moods from one another.

"You'll get used to them," Mistress Martina assured him during those first few unsettling weeks.

"Hm." He doubted that.

"You'll also have to remember they are underage. *Not enough years* might be the term you're used to."

"Yes."

"I know they are very appealing."

"Hm."

"I hope that won't become a problem for us, Yannick."

"It won't."

"See that it doesn't."

He had to do as she said. If he couldn't keep his attention and his thoughts to himself, then Mistress Martina would *let him go*, because he was the outsider. The twins were her blood.

He hardened himself, learning not to react to their presence. It wasn't so difficult, as he had a lot of practice as being self-contained.

Sometimes, the twins saw him as a challenge, but they were just as likely to forget he was there. They talked about things they probably wouldn't have mentioned in front of anyone else. Sometimes, one of them would bring him coffee, and instead of retreating, she would linger to chat to him while he kneaded or stirred.

They were accomplished scavengers, helping themselves to pinches of dough or broken biscuits.

No harm. It wasn't as if they carried any bacteria that could possibly harm the human patrons.

He'd had to learn about bacteria when he first came *over here* to the human realm.

The twins weren't flirting with him when they stole his dough. They simply acted as if he was someone they might tease now and again. As if he were a younger brother, maybe. That was what they called him, after all.

Kleiner Bruder.

In some ways, it was nice. It made him feel the warmth of family.

At the beginning, Mistress Martina had offered to help him out with references if he ever wanted to go to another job. He saw no reason to leave *Fee Kaffee* and plenty of reasons to stay. Life at the café fitted in with *Grossmutter* Agnetta's legacy. The place was a kind of home, where he could create beautiful things and look at them, too. He was good at what he did, and he saw the plates returned to the kitchen scraped and polished clean and knew he was giving satisfaction.

The girls were finally leaving. He heard their sweet voices raised in that peculiar two-part harmony they used.

"*Gute Nacht*, Tante."

Mistress Martina responded, as usual, with, "*Nacht, mädchens.*"

He liked the way they all fell into the alpenfee dialect from time to time.

Here it comes!

It was the high point of his day . . . unless it was the low point. He never really knew.

The kitchen door cracked open.

"*Gute Nacht, kleiner Bruder!*" they called, still in that two-part harmony.

Kleiner Bruder indeed! He was no one's brother and no one's son, and they were not really his family.

He heard three sets of footsteps tap across the café. The door to the street closed. The twins had gone.

Footsteps returned, and Mistress Martina opened the door and looked in at him where he stood stirring at the stove.

"Goodnight, Yannick. Don't stay on too long, now."

"Hmm."

"If you do, I'll have workplace relations people here with a *please explain why you're exploiting your baker.*"

"Hmm," he said noncommittally.

"Am I?" she asked. "Exploiting you, I mean?"

He shook his head, smelling a waft of the mocha scent that clung to her hair and skin.

She was lonely sometimes, despite the twins and people who came to the café. Her kindness troubled him. If she came too close, he might be tempted to offer her a slice of his special cake. Maybe it would work for her, if not for him.

No. It wasn't ready yet, and it wasn't the right kind of charm. In any case, feeding charmed cake to his employer would feel shady. It had to be freely asked-for, and not something he could offer.

What he was doing in the café kitchen tonight was definitely shady, but the recipe insisted on the *borrowed-in-secret* aspect.

He'd brought his own ingredients into the café on Christmas Eve and mixed the dough. He'd slipped in alone to do the second kneading on Christmas Day when the café was closed. That was secret enough. He was using Mistress Martina's oven and her tools of the trade which should take care of the *borrowed*. He also planned to use her café for his fishing expedition. The cake was the bait. The fish was — what? Only his heart's desire.

"*Dummkopf!*" he scolded himself. The twins often called one another that.

How can I hope to have a heart's desire? I mightn't even have a heart anymore.

He stirred the fruit mixture, letting the developing syrup trickle off the spoon.

Food magic had a long history, even among humans. Christmas puddings were the traditional example, with their mystique all entangled with wishes and silver coins.

Christmas puddings were common in the human realm, and he'd made a lot of them for *Fee Kaffee*.

Probably no human had ever heard of the Langel *Liebeskuchen*.

It was an old, old recipe and the only place he'd ever seen it was in the book *Grossmutter* Agnetta had cherished and had handed on to him. The recipes were all hand-lettered, and they were done in the different hands of the Langels of *Langelhame*.

He wondered how the syrup would work.

He'd got the cake base out of the oven along with the afternoon buns that he'd marked with crosses for Saint Stephen's Day.

It was well wrapped up to keep warm on the shelf with the unused cakes from today. It had been easy to slip this one into the line-up.

He frowned. One of the twins had *noticed* it while he was knocking down the dough. He hoped that didn't matter.

The syrup wasn't right.

He spotted a couple of apples on the bench. They'd been in the marketing basket and he remembered thinking it odd the twins had bought just two.

Maybe they wanted a snack and forgot to eat them. Or maybe they got them because they're from over there.

Apples from *over there* in the fay homeland were always that little bit different from the ones that grew *over here* on the human side of the gates.

He picked up the apples, one in each hand, and argued with his conscience.

If the girls had really wanted them, they would have eaten them already. Instead, they'd left them in the basket, making him an accidental present.

Maybe they were a *true* present?

When they remembered, they tried to include him in their day. They greeted him and they farewelled him, but he never managed to find a proper response that wouldn't startle them or reveal too much of *him*.

He sometimes answered them in his head.

These apples would complement the cherries he'd used. He'd had to guess about them since the recipe had called for something called *Kirschenchoice*. He didn't know that word, and since *Grossmutter* Agnetta had gone to glory, there was no one left to ask.

As far as he knew, he was the only extant twig of the Langel family tree.

That made him feel lonely.

No one had given him a gift since Agnetta handed the *Langelhame* family book into his keeping. Mistress Martina had given him a holiday bonus, but that, she'd assured him, had been earned and was part of his entitlements. He got one every year.

Maybe the twins wouldn't mind if he gifted himself with their apples . . .

Before he could change his mind, Yannick chopped the apples into confetti pieces and stirred them into his syrup.

It was ready.

He lifted it off the hob, unveiled the still-warm cherry cake and carefully sliced off the top.

Suddenly doubtful, he looked at the rosy syrup with its suspended golden flecks of apple. This could get messy.

Here goes.

He caught his intention in his mind and slowly poured the fruit into the exposed top of the cake.

He sang the lines that accompanied the recipe. "*Liebeskuchen* draw to me, *herz an herz mein lieben* key."

He hoped he had the weird blend of alpenfee dialect and English correct. There was no way the grammar was right, but charms weren't about grammar anyway.

"Charms are about intention and a sincere and loving heart, *Urenkel*." That was what Agnetta had told him. She always called him that word that meant *great-grandson*. It was as if what he was to her was more important than who.

He'd barely recognised his first name until Holly Palmer took him in hand.

He hoped he had a sincere heart and that it was loving enough to net him a life's companion. It was more than time to get the twins out of his mind and find someone to give meaning to the other part of his life that wasn't concerned with food and its creation.

"Don't you be alone, Yannick." Holly Palmer had sounded apprehensive as she kissed him goodbye.

"I'll try, Mistress Holly."

Her man, Felix, had hugged him warmly. "You're a good man, Yannick. Don't forget we're always here for you if you need us."

"*Danke*, Felix. I'll remember."

"*Lieben* key," he murmured. He supposed that meant *key to love*.

A picture came into his mind . . . not a key, but two cheerful faces.

Twins.

My twins.

Why did there have to be two of you and only one of me?

He shook them away. He told himself they had nothing to do with his venture of making a charmed cake of ancient origin and casting his lure out there on the world.

Not that he thought this would work. He supposed the recipe was made so fiendishly complicated for a reason.

Three days' work for one small cake! Secrecy. Borrowing. An impossible syrup with an intentionally missing ingredient to concoct. A difficult charm to sing. Who would bother even trying this? And if someone did try, and it didn't work, then they'd think they must have missed a step. No one would want to bother waiting a whole year and starting the sequence again on another Christmas Eve.

He emptied the syrup pan and peered at the cake, expecting it to dissolve into a mess.

It was still holding together, so he lifted the prepared lid and lowered it into place. It fitted perfectly.

Even though it wouldn't work any more than Christmas pudding luck coins worked, it would be intriguing to see who ordered his cake from the chalkboard menu.

He'd just arranged three leftover cherries on top when he heard the café door.

CHAPTER SIX: MISTLETOE MINDBENDERS

Lili, Saint Stephen's Day

After work, the twins went to the pub to consult Cèilidh Acushla on the logistics of wishing apples. They might have asked Irish Toby, but they'd have to find him first.

Nina was probably still angry with them, and they needed clarification before they tried wishing on their apples. Sometimes anger got in the way of wishes.

They rode to the *Pride of Erin* and went into the bar.

"Should we order some of her dad's poteen?" Chiara pondered aloud.

"Not on your life!"

A Christmas tree hung with paper shamrocks stood in a corner, and tinsel glittered around the walls.

Someone had hung a bunch of mistletoe over the piano.

The fatherly barman looked them over. "What's your pleasure, girls?"

"Not poteen," Chiara muttered.

"Is Cèilidh here, Master Godfrey?" Lili asked.

"She's not in tonight, Lili. Can I get you a Christmas special?"

"Yes, as long as it's not . . ." Lili began.

"Peach schnapps or poteen," Chiara finished.

The barman grinned. "A couple of Mistletoe Mindbenders coming up."

They watched as he performed the arcane ritual of shakers and bottles and flicks of the wrist.

The drinks were a pearly liquid decorated with holly leaves.

"Fresh out of mistletoe for the bar, but there's some over

the piano if you're feeling frisky," he said.

"Yes, what's with that?" Lili asked.

"It's traditional to hang mistletoe at Christmas, but these days it doesn't do to be accused of entrapment. Anyone balanced on a piano just to get under the mistletoe presumably *wants* to be kissed, and so can't raise a rumpus if it happens. That's the theory, anyway."

"You could still get into trouble if someone falls off the piano."

He made a mock frown. "There is that, of course. Obviously, having a piano that could potentially be climbed upon is a serious breach of the public safety act." He sighed. "Have to raise that with the management, maybe."

Since Master Godfrey *was* the management, there seemed to be little fear that much would change.

Lili paid and sipped her drink.

"Good?" the barman asked.

"Brilliant. Much better than the peach schnapps and poteen we had last night!"

"Trust me. *Anything* is better than that," the barman said.

"You've tried it?"

"Naturally, I have. A poor publican I'd be, sithee, if I niver took a wee nip o' me own wares, *cariad*."

"Watch out—your accent is showing."

The barman smiled, and his habitual glamour shifted a little, showing a touch of strangeness underneath before he reformed, once more, into the archetypical Aussie bloke façade he liked to display. "Which one would that be, now, young Chiara?" He turned to serve someone else before they could answer.

Lili and Chiara checked the bar for talent worth climbing a piano for. Nothing took their eye, so, after a decent interval, they set off for Dodge.

"Can't call Cèilidh. She doesn't have a phone. We'll have

to wing it," Lili said.

"We'd better get things sorted with Mum, first. At least we have the potato salad as an olive branch. Maybe it's lucky we forgot to take it home on Christmas Eve."

Lili sighed. "Dammit, we smell of Mistletoe Mindbender."

"At least it's not poteen."

"Why does she even care if we drink? It's not as if it can do us any harm."

"Not a good look," Chiara said.

Florien's car was in the drive, but not Nina's.

Reprieve, or simply putting off the inevitable? Lili wondered.

"She'll probably be feeling just as awkward about last night as we are," Chiara ventured.

"Hmph."

"Now you sound like Yannick."

Lili said, "He spoke to me. He was positively loquacious."

"What exactly did he say?"

Lili frowned. "He said, *Anything for you, my lovely.*"

"WTF?"

"That's what I thought. Do you think someone's hijacked his brain?"

They put their bikes away and let themselves in.

The house seemed abnormally silent and unnaturally empty. Florien wasn't in his study. Lili stuck her head in their brother's room, but Luca wasn't there.

"Dad?" Lili called. "Luca?"

Silence. There was no smell of cooking, either.

Lili went into the kitchen to put the potato salad away. She found Chiara gazing at the chalkboard Nina and Florien used for kitchen messages.

"Twins, Christmas catch-up with the Jasons. Plenty of leftovers in the fridge. Dad."

"Well, that explains the *Mary Celeste* look," Chiara said.

"Wish first or dinner?" Lili asked.

"Wish, I think. In our room."

Perched on her bed, Lili had a feeling of unreality. "This is mad," she said.

Chiara laughed. "Don't sweat it, *ältere Schwester*. Even if wishing doesn't get us out of Dodge, we're due for a bit of fun."

"It's a sign of how lacking our social lives are when the best thing we can think of to do of a Saturday evening is to share two apples thrown to us by a blarney-tongued man at the market." She sighed. "We didn't even get kissed under the mistletoe at the pub."

"Would you rather not do this?"

Lili raised her chin. "I rather *would*."

Chiara said, "Better cut those apples up. We have to share them, not each eat our own. Then we make our wishes together, and we service one another's."

Lili waited expectantly but a slight frown flitted over her twin's face.

"What?"

"Lil, do you have my apple?"

"No, of —"

She felt her face mirror her sister's as she realised she didn't have her apple, either.

"Dammit, we must have left them at the firm."

Chiara bounced up. "We'll have to go and get them."

"We could leave it until tomorrow."

"No, *Schwester*. By then we'll start second-guessing ourselves. And remember, the farther out from Christmas, the weaker the wish."

In three minutes they were heading back to *Fee Kaffee*.

"Let's hope we didn't leave them at the market," Lili said.

"We couldn't have."

"No. Irish tossed them to both of us, and then I blew him his kiss," Lili recalled.

"You flirt, Lili!"

"And then he did the blarney thing about the wish, and then . . ."

"I blew him his kiss."

"You flirt, Chiara!"

"And he graciously included me in the wish thing. Why does everyone deal with you first?"

"I'm older."

"Ten minutes. Never mind. And he said—"

"Wish gift for a kiss, girleens!" Lili said. "And I said . . ."

"You asked him where the wish was, and he said it was the apple."

"No, *I* said that."

"But then *he* said . . ."

"Be sure to share it with the other parties," they said together.

"And then we did—what?"

"I think we must have put them in the market baskets, because if we'd eaten them, we'd remember, and if we'd stuffed them in our pockets, they'd still be there, and they're not," Lili said.

They rounded a corner and pulled up at *Fee Kaffee*.

"No need to bother *Tante*," Lili said.

"We can just duck into the kitchen and get the apples and then go home."

"No, let's do the wish right here."

Chiara grabbed her hand. "Perfect! This is much more *us* than Dodge, and besides, you never know when Mum and Dad might show up. We'd never hear the last of it if Mum caught us in mid-wish."

Holding hands, they let themselves into *Fee Kaffee*.

The sun had set, and the inside of the café was dusky. Lili

hesitated to switch on the lights, in case it attracted would-be customers who would be disappointed.

"Dirndls," Chiara said.

"Yes. More *us*. More wishy."

With the ease of three years of practice, they conjured their work uniforms from the rail in the staffroom.

"Okay, where are those apples?"

Lili sighed. "Why didn't we just conjure them instead of coming all the way back here? They're ours, after all."

"I did try that while we were getting our bikes, *Dummkopf*. I used the basket as a fix, but it didn't work."

They checked, anyway, but the big marketing baskets were empty.

"Yannick must have taken them out when he unloaded the baskets."

"Might be in the larder." Chiara went to see.

Lili heard her sister give a pleased *oooh!* "Got them?"

"No, but this you *have* to see!"

Lili went into the larder and squinted through the twilight. She clicked her fingers to bring up a lamp and blinked as she saw what Chiara had found.

"*Gott im Himmel!* Will you look at that cake!"

"Isn't it glorious?" Chiara leaned over to sniff. "Cherries! And there's something else. Like candied peel, but not. Is that figs? It's still warm!"

Lili breathed in the enticing scent. Her mouth watered. "Do you think we could have some?"

"*Tante* always says we can eat what we like—in reason."

"That's during working hours."

"I *wish* things didn't have to be so complicated," Chiara said.

"Well, *I* wish we could find those wish apples and get what we want."

Chiara sighed. "Yes, but you know what I wish for right

now?"

Lili's mouth was still watering, so she had a pretty good idea.

Together the twins chorused, "Some of that cake."

CHAPTER SEVEN: MERRY CHRISTMAS, LOVELIES

Yannick, Saint Stephen's Day

When the café door opened, Yannick's first instinct was to hide.

He couldn't fit in the oven, and anyway, that had nasty connotations of *Hansel and Gretel*. He shot into the staffroom.

The twins' dirndls were there, and he wondered why they didn't keep them at home.

He held his breath, hearing approaching footsteps.

It was the twins. He smelled their light perfume through the closed door. Apples and cherries . . . just like his Langel *Liebeskuchen*.

No – no – what?

His brain went into overdrive.

What are they doing here?

Apples and cherries . . .

What have I done?

He was crouched near the door and a sudden movement in the dimness caught his attention.

The dirndls vanished, leaving their cotton covers deflated.

He listened to those familiar voices, murmuring together until one of them suddenly exclaimed.

"This you *have* to see!"

Yannick knew exactly what they'd found.

He could stay hidden in the staffroom, but what if they —

He straightened up.

Grossmutter . . . help me.

She wasn't there. Only he was there. And the Langel *Liebeskuchen*. And the twins.

He opened the door and edged back into the kitchen.

It was almost dark, but he saw lamplight seeping through the larder door.

"I *wish* things didn't have to be so complicated."

That was one of the—*Ow!* Yannick shied as the wish hit him front and centre.

"Well, *I* wish we could find those wish apples and get what we want."

"Yes, but you know what I wish for right now?"

"Some of that cake."

He felt winded, but everything complicated unravelled in his mind. It was like the childhood feeling of sitting in a tightly wound swing and letting it spin rapidly back to normal.

He walked to the larder and conjured open the door.

Two startled young women turned to face him. Their colour was high and each of them held a slice of his charmed cake. Their eyes looked guilty and enormous.

They were—

Adorable.

His.

There are two of them.

I don't care.

He said quickly, with the words falling over one another, "It's all *right*, my lovelies. It's for you. It's yours. Ours. It's your apples—my—your—" He saw their eyes widen and his voice broke into a stammer.

What have I done? They haven't eaten it yet!

Chiara lifted her free hand, broke a corner of the cake and put the crumb in her mouth.

He said, "Stop!"

They blinked.

"What the fuck is going on?" Lili said. She was staring at him as if he was—

"You said we could eat it," Chiara reproached him,

breaking off another morsel. She added, "You're talking. Lili, he's totally talking. You were right."

"Yes, you can have it, but I have to tell you first. Disclose. It's charmed."

They went on staring at him.

"We *know* that, *Dummkopf*," Lili said.

Chiara asked, "Have you seen our apples, Yannick?"

"If you mean those spare apples from the marketing baskets, they're in there." He indicated the cake.

"They weren't spare."

"They were ours."

"You used our Christmas wish apples in your charmed cake?" Chiara said.

He nodded, cringing inwardly.

Lili said, "In that case, we'll *have* to eat it. Otherwise, we'll never get out of Dodge."

She raised the cake to her lips and bit in. "This ish— ummmmm . . .

Yannick watched helplessly as her eyes lit up. "I have to explain."

Chiara gave up on small pieces and bit the end off her slice. "Explain away." She rescued a dab of syrup with her tongue.

Lili licked her fingers and nodded to the remaining cake on the board. "You'd better get cracking if you want some. Otherwise, we'll eat it all."

He hesitated. The recipe implied he should observe to see who came for the cake and then make her acquaintance. It didn't suggest whether or not he should eat any.

Lili smiled at him. "Yannick, you're one of the other parties. You've got to share our wish apples, and since you've stolen them and stuck them in this cake . . ." She picked up the silver knife they must have used to slice it and cut off a generous piece. "Are you going to eat this of your own free will, or are we going to have to hold you down and sit on you until you do what we want?"

Oh . . .

He put out his hand and accepted the slice she gave him.

All that syrup . . . where did it go? Sit on me? Gott im Himmel!

He took a bite and chewed, watching the twins nervously. He felt as if his eyes might be rolling like those of a panicked horse.

Lili said, "What is this, exactly?"

He said, "It's called Langel *Liebeskuchen.*"

"Langel . . . as in your name? You invented it? If you can do this, why the devil are you working at a café in a regional town?"

"It's a family recipe." He told them about Agnetta's battered book, which now belonged to him.

"I had to vary the recipe because it has ingredients I couldn't translate."

"Including stolen apples," Lili said.

"Not really stolen. The syrup needed something extra and they were *there.*"

Chiara leaned over the cake. "There's enough for three more pieces. That's if we can have some more?"

"Anything for you, my lovelies," he said.

Chiara cut the cake and held out one of the pieces.

Lili stared at him and then turned to her sister. "See? He said it. I told you he said it. He totally said it."

"I what?"

"That's what you said when I asked if I could have a ginger biscuit. After you hid your cake dough from me."

He opened his mouth to deny saying any such thing, but then the scene replayed in his mind.

"I didn't say that. Not aloud," he said.

They both refocused on him.

"You do it, too . . ."

"The talking thing where you say . . ."

"What you want to say but can't say it . . ."

"Aloud."

"It's lucky I have three years of experience at dealing with twin-talk," he said.

He ate the rest of his slice, noting the twins had already finished theirs.

"That was the best . . ."

"Cake we ever . . ."

"Stole," he said, finishing their sentence.

"You *said* – "

Chiara put her hand on Lili's arm. "You think our wish apples will work incorporated into the cake?"

Lili looked dismayed. "I think we were meant to make the wish *before* we ate them.

"You did," Yannick said.

They turned to him round-eyed, obviously seeking explanations.

"You wished to uncomplicate your lives, and to find your apples and to get what you want."

"Oh."

"And you think – "

"What we want – "

"Is *you?*"

"Let's find out. Come here," he said, and he held out his arms.

The twins, moving in harmony, as usual, came closer. As they stepped up, they put their arms around one another and their other arms around him. He leaned his face down between theirs, feeling their soft cheeks on his. He was wrapped in the summery smell of apples and cherries.

His heart lurched, but he sighed in contentment. "Merry Christmas, lovelies."

They moved closer, and one of them said, "He totally can speak . . ."

"If he wants to," the other said.

"Probably he always did want to . . ."

"Only the words never made it . . ."

"Outside his head."

Lili said, "What are we calling you?"

This time he knew which one was speaking and his new clarity told him that was because she was speaking *to* him rather than *about* him.

"You'd better use my name, my lovely Lili."

Chapter Eight: Going Home

Lili, Saint Stephen's Day

Lili breathed in deeply. She smelled Chiara's scent, which was like her own, and the warm mix of baking spice which came from Yannick.

The three-way hug felt wonderfully right.

"Why didn't we ever do this before?" she asked Chiara.

"Eat charmed cake, or cuddle *Tante* Martina's baker in the larder?"

"This," she said, tightening her arms as emphasis.

She added, to Yannick, "We've been trawling about for ages, trying to find a pair of men to suit us."

"But either they're creepy-peculiar," Chiara said.

"Or they think *we're* creepy-peculiar," Lili finished.

"And we're not."

"And we even rejected some perfectly nice lads . . ."

"Such as Dylan Castle . . ."

"Who totally wants to get in Lili's pants . . ."

"Because there was only one of him."

"So why didn't we just decide to share one before?" Chiara asked plaintively.

Lili raised her head and tilted it back so she could see their grumpy baker. "You look shocked, Yannick. I hope you don't mind being shared?"

"No," he said. His arms tightened, and he said, "Apparently, it's my heart's desire to be shared."

They stood there for a while in silence, and then Yannick said, "I have to tell you some important things, and I don't want to do it here."

"Why not?"

"Probably because there isn't a bed here," Chiara said.

Lili felt Yannick give a nervous jolt at that. "I hope you're not going to be precious about this, *kleiner —* " She broke off and then said, "Yannick, I mean. Sharing means *sharing,* and that means doing some nice things in bed. Where do you want to talk, if not here? We do have beds, but they're just king singles. There's no way we'd be able to get all three of us in one."

"It could be done if we did a kind of club sandwich. Twin bread with a baker filling," Chiara suggested.

"You can't sleep like that," Lili objected. She added, "Anyway, if we go to Dodge, things will be complicated again, and we only just got them uncomplicated."

"Yannick uncomplicated them," Chiara said.

Yannick said, "Let's do it at home."

"Home? We just told you — "

"Our home," he said.

"Sounds like a plan," Lili said, on a rush of relief.

Home. Definitely, home was where they should go.

"Now?" Chiara asked.

"Almost now." Yannick's embrace slackened.

Lili moved forward. "Don't do that."

"We have things to do, lovelies." He sounded unexpectedly firm.

"What things?"

He stepped away, pulled a phone from his pocket and checked the display. "It's getting on for nine, and I'm due back here at three."

"That won't work," Chiara said.

"No," Lili agreed.

"I have to get the bread on at three."

"Isn't there a quicker bread you can make?" Lili asked.

"*Eierbrot.*" Yannick stepped into the larder.

"Now, what are you doing?"

"Alpenfee egg-bread. It's a quick bread, and I think

43

Mistress Martina would allow it out of season just for once. I can set the ingredients out now." As he spoke, he was assembling bulk ingredients. "Buttermilk?"

Chiara went to get it.

"Beer."

Lili brought a bottle.

"Rye flour . . . and eggs. They ought to be goose eggs, but hen will have to do. Can you put fourteen in a basin?"

Lili went to get the eggs while Chiara located one of the big bowls. She plucked an unused Christmas napkin from the pile of clean tablecloths, and on a whim, she conjured a marker from the staffroom.

She flattened the napkin on the bench. "Hold this straight, will you?" she asked, and her twin obligingly took hold of the corners.

Lili considered a moment and then wrote *Just Eloped* on the white centre. Then she held the napkin while Chiara drew an emphatic heart around the words.

"What are we doing with this?" Chiara asked.

Lili held her finger to her lips. "Surprise for Yannick when he starts the bread in the morning," she whispered. She pushed the napkin into the china bowl and hurriedly piled the eggs on top.

Chiara put her head on one side. "It needs something to decorate it. A bow?"

Lili shook her head, and then she conjured one of the packing feathers from the eggbox. "Perfect!"

"Are you ready for home, lovelies?" Yannick called.

"Ready," they chorused.

They still had no idea where they were going, but they trusted it was somewhere nice.

Yannick doused the lantern and checked the kitchen before leading them through into the garage. He conjured the door of the van open.

"Jump in the back."

"Why? Are you kidnapping us?" Chiara suggested.

"You won't both fit in the front and I can't drive if I'm distracted."

They got in the back seat.

Yannick backed out of the garage and conjured the doors closed. "Are you lovelies sure about this?"

They exchanged glances in the darkness.

"Are we?" Chiara asked.

Lili thought about it. Then she said, "We're getting out of Dodge and we're going home to be his lovelies."

That said it all.

CHAPTER NINE: LANGELHAME

Chiara, Saint Stephen's Day Night

Chiara sat clutching Lili's hand in the back of a van.
"We're eloping with the baker."

Lili said, "Yes. Isn't it perfect?"

The sides of the van were enclosed, which meant they couldn't see out. That didn't matter. They trusted they'd get where they needed to be.

Suddenly, Chiara remembered something. "We'll have to go back! We left our bikes propped outside the firm door!"

"So we'll conjure them somewhere safe."

"Not into the garage . . . might scratch *Tante*'s car."

"Back to Dodge," Chiara decided. It was the only place she could think of.

Yannick will have to drive us back to Dodge in the morning to get them.

We're not going back, really. Not to live. Only to visit.

They drove on for a few minutes, and then Yannick slowed and pulled into a parking spot.

"Are we home yet?" Chiara asked.

"No, but this is where we leave the van. We have to walk the rest."

The twins climbed out and looked up at a dimly lit building.

"Grene Motor Clinic," Chiara read. She began to have an inkling of where they were going. "We live in the Peckerdale-Grene tower? Nice!"

"Not there." Yannick caught their hands and led them away from the garage and across a green belt area in the dark. The Peckerdale-Grene tower community lay to their left, and ahead crouched a dark grove of trees.

"We're going *over there*," Chiara said to Lili.

Over there was the fay homeland. Martina went there now and again, to visit friends, but it was a long while since the twins had been through the gates. Nina didn't approve.

The dark copse swallowed them, and the scent of flowers and leaves breathed in the night, cutting them off from the human realm as the Peckerdale-Grene wards embraced them.

They were already holding hands, with Yannick in the middle, so it fell to Chiara to open the gate. Since she didn't know their destination, she disengaged her expectation, concentrating instead on the warmth of a man's hand holding hers.

It certainly wasn't damp.

The latch, which was both there and not there, lifted easily, and she stepped forwards, feeling the others follow.

The gate closed behind them, the perspective changed, and the air was suddenly cooler with a fresh scent of pine and spruce.

"Where are we?" Lili asked.

Chiara breathed deeply in air that would never be touched by petrol.

"Nordalp, it's called," Yannick said.

"Nordalp," Chiara said, trying the word in her mouth.

We live in Nordalp.

Yannick went on explaining, "It's probably nowhere you've been before. It's out-of-the-way, an enclave between the alpenfolk and fjordfee homelands. Home is just up the slope, but you can't see it from here."

Still holding hands, they climbed a narrow pathway, and the air grew steadily cooler. Chiara shivered.

Should have brought my jacket.

There was no use thinking of that. She couldn't conjure clothing through the gate.

"It's just a step along," Yannick said.

They came up through a cleft in the alp and onto a flat area where a dark building backed against the rock.

It looked forbidding.

Yannick stopped and let go of their hands. "Here we are."

"*Gott im Himmel!* We're going to live in Drac's Castle!" Lili whispered.

Yannick said, "I suppose it might strike you like that." He conjured open the door and hesitated. "I can't carry you both over the threshold."

"You could take us one by one," Chiara said.

"But that would mean choosing one of you first and I never could do that."

Chiara put that away to unpack later. Generally, folk had no trouble choosing which was first and which was second. She was always second.

"Let's go hand-in-hand," she said.

Yannick reached out, and Chiara retook his hand. They climbed a short flight of stone stairs and stepped into the hall.

Yannick conjured the door closed behind them. "Straight through the inner hanging," he said, stepping away.

Chiara anchored herself to the familiar comfort of Lili's hand, and they edged forward through a gap between two heavy cloth drapes. The room they entered was much warmer, and they saw the deep glow of a banked fireplace.

Yannick came in behind them and snapped his fingers to bring up the lamps.

Chiara closed her eyes reflexively as the light hit her, but Lili's gasp alerted her to open them again.

The room was a jewel box of rich colour with woven hangings on the wall and carved furniture painted and gilded with fantastic patterns of cherry red and gold.

Yannick was at the fireplace, breaking turves apart to let in some air, but he turned to look at them somewhat defensively. "I know it's a bit—"

"Whoa!" Chiara turned slowly, gazing at the huge room. "It's *gorgeous!*"

"It's like that cake, only made to live in," Lili said.

Yannick blew out his cheeks. "You'll accept it as home, then?"

"We already did, when we accepted you," Chiara said. She sat down on a low couch, which configured itself to her weight. "What's this stuffed with?"

"Wool from the *alpenziegen . . .* the fay goats hereabouts. Well, they're almost goats. *Grossmutter* said they'd crossed with some of the sheep from the lower alps."

"*Grossmutter?* The one with the recipes?" Lili asked. She sat down at the other end of the couch.

Chiara was about to move closer when she realised Lili had left room for Yannick.

He was still standing near the fireplace, so she patted the seat. "You said you had important things to tell us," she reminded.

Yannick said, "I do." He came to sit, and Chiara wiggled in close until he put his arm around her.

Ahhh.

It was already feeling natural and even necessary.

That was something else to unpack, maybe when she unpacked Yannick.

She rested her head against his shoulder, aware of Lili settling likewise on his other side. She hitched her hip so she could curve closer.

"Go on," she murmured.

"This house is called *Langelhame,*" Yannick said. "I don't know who built it, and I wasn't born here. The first thing I really do remember is living here with Agnetta. I called her *Grossmutter,* but she was my great-grandmother, really."

"What about your parents?" Lili asked.

"I don't know. Agnetta never said much about them. A tal

came to see us every so often. He said he was my uncle, and I think he probably was. Agnetta called him Enkel, which wasn't much use."

That meant *grandson,* Chiara knew.

"His name wasn't Langel. I think he lived in Germany. He wasn't from *over here,* anyway and I think he came to see us out of duty. He's the one who talked *Grossmutter* into getting me sponsored *over there,* in Shipley . . . you know Shipley?"

"Yes, it's a good way down the coast. There's a lighthouse there. We've always wanted to climb it," Lili said.

"I think the reason my uncle picked it was because it was too far from the gateway for me to bolt back home.

"I went to live with some people named Palmer. They sponsor a lot of us from *over here,* and they were so kind to me. My uncle and Agnetta didn't get along well, but they both wanted what was best for me, although I didn't understand that at the time. After I went to Shipley, I didn't see my uncle again.

"When *the slip* started for *Grossmutter,* someone sent a message to Holly — Mistress Palmer — and I came home.

"Agnetta gave me the family recipe book. She said as long as I lived here in this house, I would have tree rule and a home, and that I was to *hold heritage.* Do you *mädchens* know what tree rule is?"

Chiara said doubtfully, "Not really."

"It's a habitation right. If anyone *over here* grows trees for seven years or makes a garden or curates a flock . . . anything like that . . . and no one objects, then that place belongs to them until or unless they abandon it for another seven years. I've lived in *Langelhame* ever since I remember, so it's my home." His arm tightened. "Yours, too, now, my lovelies."

Chiara digested this. She realised that because the Blesses and Nina's family, the Lucans, had *lived human* for so long, there were bound to be things they didn't know about how things worked *over here.*

"So you've lived in this house alone since your great-grandmother died?"

"I have. When she was young, she worked at one of the courtlands manors as a head baker. She came back here when her father passed, and this is where she was when she took me in. At least, I think so." He caught his breath. "Is there anything you want to know?"

"How did you come to work for *Tante* Martina?" Lili asked.

"She didn't tell you?"

"No. As far as we know, you applied for the job the way anyone else might do."

"I did apply. Holly Palmer said having an *over there* identity might come in handy, so she let me know when she heard Mistress Martina was looking for a baker. They don't know one another, but she knew Patterdale was a good place for me to be."

"Do you see much of her and her family?" Chiara asked.

"Not now. As you said, they're a good way down the coast, and they're busy. They run a kind of holiday home. I could drive down to Shipley during my off-shift, but it wouldn't leave me a lot of time to sleep."

Chiara tried to imagine what life had been like for Yannick for the past few years. It made her and Lili's *Get out of Dodge* problem look petty in comparison. That was yet another thing to unpack when she had time. She saw she was going to be busy arranging things in her head.

Yannick said, abruptly, "Are you hungry?"

"No," Chiara said. She was aware of Lili's voice saying the same thing.

"It must be the cake. We haven't had dinner, but we usually go to bed quite early anyway, because of doing the marketing," Lili said.

CHAPTER TEN: BED FOR THREE

Lili, Saint Stephen's Day Night

It had been an eventful day, and it wasn't over yet.

Lili conjured her phone out of the pocket of her dirndl and tapped the screen.

It was dark.

"That won't work here," Yannick said.

Of course it wouldn't. Lili felt foolish. She knew perfectly well motors and electronics didn't work *over here* in the fay homelands. That was the reason their friend Cèilidh Acushla didn't bother with a phone.

"You can't check your socials here," Chiara said.

"It wasn't that—it was the time."

"I should think it's well after ten," Chiara reasoned.

"Definitely time for bed, then," Lili said. She felt an odd jolt of excitement.

No one moved, so Lili gently extricated herself from the crook of Yannick's arm. "Where do we sleep? Is the loo outside?"

"It's through there with the tub," Yannick said, nodding towards a door half-hidden by one of the hangings.

"We'll go and have a wash before bed, then. Where *is* the bed?"

Yannick indicated the foot of a stairway in the corner of the room.

"Okay, we'll come to you there when we've cleaned up." She held out her hands to Chiara and pulled her to her feet.

The bathroom was nothing like the one in Dodge or at the café, but after a bit of consideration, they worked out the pump system and what they thought might be called an earth closet.

"We don't have our toothbrushes," Chiara said.

"Or any other clothes." Lili sat on the edge of the round tub and started to laugh. "We didn't manage our elopement very efficiently. Oh, well. We can easily get our things when we go back to the firm."

They contemplated one another and then said, together, "Are you sorry we did this?"

"No!" Chiara said.

"Neither am I."

"Why were you bothering about the time, then?"

Lili shrugged. "It's been a long day, and—"

"We have an eloped-with and possibly terrified baker to share."

"And I think we need to do that while it's still Saint Stephen's Day."

"It's not just a one-night-deal though," Chiara said.

"No. We live here now. Yannick said so. But that cake—"

"Langel *Liebeskuchen*—"

"Yes. Yannick made it over three days. There are three of us. That seems to be significant and so—"

"We need to do what?"

"I *think* maybe we need to spend three days—um—"

"Consolidating?"

"Yes."

"Let's go and consolidate our baker, then."

"Yannick."

"Yes, I know . . . but he calls us *lovelies*."

"Well, we *are* lovely."

"And he's a baker."

They returned to the main room, where the lamps were lowered and the fire banked down.

The foot of the stair was only just visible. Lili pushed aside a hanging and looked up. "It's a spiral, like the one *Tante*

Martina has in her house," she observed.

She began to climb the unfamiliar stair.

At the top, yet another hanging screened the landing, and Lili ducked through and stopped dead with surprise.

Behind her, she heard Chiara say, "Whoa!"

She didn't know what they'd expected, but what they saw was a kind of half-room, jutting out over the main floor. A mezzanine, she thought it was called.

The space was made from polished wood, and it was dominated by the biggest bed she had ever seen.

Tante Martina had a big feather bed . . . but the one in *Langelhame* was enormous.

Yannick lay in the middle.

"Whoa!" Chiara said again.

"We certainly don't have to worry about how you're going to fit us into that one," Lili said. She conjured off her dirndl and hesitated in her bra and knickers.

Yannick raised one hand and clicked his fingers, plunging the bed floor into the moonlight, which flowed down from a skylight Lili hadn't noticed before.

Better.

Lili shed the rest of her clothing and climbed in, aware of Chiara doing the same on the other side. For a few seconds, it felt strange. The bed was evidently stuffed with the same wool as the couch downstairs. The pillows and linen smelled of sunshine and fresh air. It was as different from her single bed in Dodge as she could imagine any bed would be.

For one thing, it had an eloped-with baker in the middle.

Our bed. Our baker. Ours.

She rolled in to face Chiara over the top of their baker.

"Have you thought—"

"How this sharing thing—"

"Is going to work?"

"I mean—do we—"

"Kiss him—"

"Or — what?"

"Maybe we should have worked this out — "

"Let's just get on with it while it's still Saint Stephen's Day," Lili said.

She put her hand on Yannick's chest and bent to kiss him, but in the dark, she missed and bumped her head. She realised Chiara must have had the same idea at the same time.

"He's only got one mouth," she said.

"Yes, but he's got a cock as well."

"So we each get something delicious to play with?"

"That'll totally work," Chiara said brightly.

Yannick sat up. "Don't I get a say in this, my lovelies?"

"Of course you do." Lili pushed him flat and shoved the bedclothes down the bed.

"Ooh, pretty," Chiara cooed.

"I'm not — "

"Not sloppy, and not greyish . . ."

"His hair down there's dark, though. Has he got teg in him?"

"Stop that!" The yell from their baker made them both freeze.

Lili felt a chill of dismay. The elopement that had seemed so perfect looked as if it was about to become derailed.

Chapter Eleven: Consolidation

Yannick, Saint Stephen's Day Night

Yannick felt his lovely twins go still as if he'd slapped them.

"What's wrong?" Lili asked. Her voice wobbled.

"Nothing." He tried to keep his tone light while gritting his teeth.

"Why did you want us to stop, then? We do know what to do and what goes where," Chiara said.

"Um—do you?" Lili ventured.

It was a fair question, but he said, "I do."

In theory, anyway.

There hadn't been a lot of chance to experiment since he'd been working at the café.

"While you're describing me and pondering my ancestry and—" He dragged in a breath and his head spun from the sweetness of apples and cherries that hung about them.

"He's gone all limp—" Lili began.

"No!" Yannick blurted.

"Oh, now he's—"

"No!"

Finally, they stopped.

"Please listen to me," he said, more moderately.

There was no answer, but he heard them stirring uneasily.

His brain fought to get the message.

I'm in bed with my beautiful twins. They're naked, and they're willing. Those lovely bodies are just waiting for me to explore. This is my heart's desire and their wish. So why am I being —

He heard a gentle intake of breath from either side of him.

"Oh, he's doing it again!"

"Totally talking in his—"

Silence.

Then, Lili said, aloud, "We *can* sort of hear you when you do that. It started after I got my fingers into your dough."

"He doesn't like it when—" one of them said, then broke off. "I mean *you* don't like it when we talk to one another about you?"

He lay down cautiously. "I'm used to your twin-babble, but I'm not used to it being about me." *And especially not about the state of my cock.*

"We're not used to you *talking* at all," Lili pointed out.

"I never managed to get anything out of my head, as you said."

"You're talking now."

He said, carefully, "Talk to one another all you like, but remember, I'm here. If you want to speculate about why I have dark hair down there, then ask me, not one another. I mightn't have answers, but I *am* here."

He felt one twin . . . Chiara . . . squirm down, and then he felt her warm breath on his thighs. She stroked her fingers through his thatch of hair.

"It is dark for an alpenfee man. Are you all alpenfee, Yannick? Not that it matters a scrap if you're not."

"I understand I am, but who knows? I'm not even sure where I was born."

She bent lower, and he felt her lips brush over his cock in a whisper-light caress.

Lili curled beside him and pulled his head against her firm breasts.

He nuzzled in gratefully and sucked one of the offered nipples.

She murmured with pleasure, and Chiara pushed a hand up to grasp one of his.

He stroked her hair as she continued to kiss his cock.

He swallowed, spacing out in pleasure given and received.

His lovelies were squirming against him, and he felt their excitement growing.

How are we going to —

Ah!

He realised they had given him the answer in their previous twin-babble.

His mouth was busy, and his cock felt ready to express itself in some messy and explosive fashion . . .

One mouth and one cock.

He sent their words back to them.

That can pleasure all of us. Remember, you threatened to sit on me until I did what you wanted? Do that now.

Lili had been writhing against his mouth, drawing great gulps of air.

Chiara was sucking him, still clinging to his hand. A shiver ran through him.

"Now!" he managed to say.

There was a scramble, and both twins got up to straddle him, one over his mouth and the other over his saliva-drenched cock.

They lowered themselves slowly, and the movements began again.

Lili tasted as delightful as she smelled, and Chiara's juices were squelching as she rocked against him, with her firm thighs embracing his flanks.

He thrust tongue and cock together in rhythm, and suddenly everything went still for a second before the girls squealed in unison in a long, wavering two-part harmony.

He had hardly time to appreciate it before his control broke into waves. He was aware of Lili sliding off, clearing his mouth just in time for him to yell in exultation.

When the maelstrom had ended, he was lying against his pillows, with a warm, damp twin on either side. Each had a leg thrown over him in a possessive fashion. One was stroking his chest while the other was dreamily sucking his shoulder.

Ahhhh.

Lili stopped sucking and nipped.

"Ouch!"

"That's the second yelp out of you," she said, sounding pleased.

"First. It's only the first time you bit me."

He hoped she might do it again.

"You yelped when you shot," Chiara said. She rubbed her fingers across his belly. "Did you remember to hold?"

"I hope so."

"So do I."

"Did *you*, Chi?" Lili asked. She didn't sound too troubled.

"I remembered just before he — just before Yannick yelped. I hope I did it right. Uncle Dario sort of explained, remember?"

"What?" Yannick said, rather appalled.

"Uncle Dario is Dad and *Tante* Martina's younger brother," Lili said.

"He told us about *holding hard* when we turned eighteen," Chiara explained.

"Because he said Mum wouldn't — "

"And he thought we should know — "

"Because we were probably going to be very sexy — "

"Women, and he wanted us to — "

"Be happy and safe — "

"And not have little oopsies until we were ready."

"He wasn't being creepy-peculiar," Lili assured.

"Just practical. It sounded odd, and Uncle Dario is an egger-onner, so we checked the facts with *Tante* Martina — "

"And she laughed and said, yes, that was quite true, but that he'd know more than she would."

"Then she told us a few things about yodelling."

Lili giggled. "It made her blush. We asked Uncle Dario and — "

"Oh, dear!" Chiara broke into laughter.

She wriggled her fingers lower and fondled Yannick's cock. "To get back to yelping, you should totally do it every time you get yours, but maybe you could manage to sound off a few seconds earlier to give us the signal to *hold*."

"I didn't need to worry about that, this time," Lili said smugly.

"Neither will I, next time. Maybe."

Yannick felt the warmth of wellbeing in his blood. He decided he'd be glad the twins had this Uncle Dario to talk to. If he was like Mistress Martina, he must be a good person. He tightened his arms, drawing his twins close. "You yodelled together."

"Mm," Chiara said.

Lili nipped him again. "Oh. No yelp this time."

"I'm about yelped out, my lovelies."

Belatedly, he remembered his manners, as explained to him by the matter-of-fact Holly Palmer when he was seventeen and about to go home to be with *Grossmutter* Agnetta for her last few days.

You're not to be alone, Yannick. Now listen, while I tell you some secrets about how to be the good man you are when you have lovers. First off, observe the courtesies . . . and remember your manners . . .

He said, "If you get off my arms, I can conjure you some warm damp cloths for cleaning up. I'll show you where things are kept in the morning, and then you'll be able to do it yourselves if you want to. Or, I can always do it."

Grumbling, they eased away, and he managed to focus enough to conjure the cloths.

He heard giggling and dabbling, and then one twin wiped him down. That felt extraordinary. He thought Agnetta had probably bathed and dried him when he was a tiddler, but he didn't remember that. He was sure she'd have done it efficiently, with a rough-dried towel.

The other twin, Lili, said, "I've refolded my cloth so I can wipe your face."

"*Danke,* Lili. *Danke,* Chiara," he said.

He felt more pats and dabs of a cloth, and when it finished, he said, "Are you hungry now? Thirsty?"

"No." They spoke together.

"I will be when I wake up," Lili said thoughtfully.

"But just now we're too tired . . ."

"So we'd just slop the tea in the bed."

Yannick conjured away the cloths and pulled up the bed-clothes. His twins settled against him again and made identical snuggling movements before they relaxed.

He relaxed as well.

He was almost entirely happy, but he was also acutely aware of how late it was and how early it very soon would be.

Then, thankfully, he remembered the *eierbrot,* the alpenfee Easter egg-bread. He'd laid out all the ingredients ready for a later morning start. That could be made quickly and baked without the trouble of multiple rising and kneading.

Mentally, he added two hours to his available window for sleep.

His last thought was that Mistress Martina would probably not grudge him a little extra personal time.

It wasn't every night a man eloped.

Only . . . he'd eloped with his lovelies, and they were her nieces.

And she'd made it gently plain that they were off-limits.

CHAPTER TWELVE: LOVE IN THE MORNING

Yannick, December Twenty-seventh

Yannick stirred. He felt uncommonly rested and uncommonly warm.

He smelled the delicious bouquet of cherries and apples that had haunted and tempted him ever since he first laid eyes on Mistress Martina's twin nieces.

He inhaled rapturously.

It was quiet, but not quite as silent as most of his awakenings. Gentle breathing whispered in his ears on either side. He was *not* alone.

He opened his eyes and looked left. A sheet of wheat-fair hair spilled over his shoulder and over the breasts of the girl beside him.

My lovely Chiara.

He rolled his head slowly and looked right.

My lovely Lili. Her hair was a little darker . . . a warm, soft ash brown.

They were beautiful, and both of them were his.

His cock twitched and he flicked his gaze down nervously. Then he relaxed. That was perfectly in order.

Lili sighed, and he glanced her way in time to see her soft pink lips curve and part as if she were enjoying her dreams.

I could suck the lower one, and then I might —

"And what about me?"

Chiara was watching him from narrowed grey eyes.

"I was thinking I might kiss your waist, just above your hip." It was true, although he'd only just thought it.

"Nice save, Yannick." She smiled.

A hand brushed his thigh and began to fondle his hip. "Is there anything particular you would like to do this morning?" Lili asked.

He snapped his head around and saw her also smiling at him, blue eyes as clear as if she hadn't been asleep a few seconds ago.

"Lots of things," he said, frankly.

"Me, too. I'd like to have a good look at you in daylight."

"Moonlight and firelight are romantic," Chiara said.

"But daylight will let us appreciate you more, in finer detail."

"It's not as if—"

"We've ever had a good chance—"

"To look at a pretty cock—"

"Before."

"I wouldn't call it pretty," he said cautiously.

Chiara peeled down the bedcovers and dropped a gentle kiss on him. "It's pretty. It's *beautiful*. Seems a shame to hide it where the sun don't shine, but I'd like to practise *holding* again to make sure I get it right," she announced.

"Breakfast first. I'm hungry," Lili said. She kissed him.

"You can have breakfast while I'm having Yannick," Chiara said.

Yannick waited for the objection, but Lili rolled out of bed. "Do you have something I could put on?" she asked.

"There are bed-shirts in the press." He pointed.

"*Danke.*" She opened the press and put on a red one with what he considered was excessive wriggling. It looked spectacularly better on her than it did on him. "Kitchen?" she asked.

"Downstairs and through the door behind the green hanging. Have whatever you want."

Lili leaned over and kissed his nose. "I'm not abandoning you, Yannick. I'm just hungry. I knew I would be. I'll eat something, and then I'll make some tea and bring it up a bit later." She went down the stairs.

Chiara snuggled up. "We thought it would be nice to share you this way, too." She stroked him again, and then she continued, "But then we thought maybe you'd feel tired, so if you'd rather, cuddling is something else we never get much of a chance at."

Cuddling was something he *never* usually got a chance at.

"Maybe we can do both," he said.

He was greedy for the touch of skin on skin and he was eager to explore the lovely contours of his lovelies.

"Cuddle first or after?" Chiara asked.

"Both?" he said hopefully.

"Nice. Perfect."

They kissed, and the *both* ensued with enough warmth and enthusiasm to make the proceedings noisy.

They were well into the *after* cuddling when Lili returned, carrying a tray of rye bread and butter, tea, and three ripe pears. "Where did you hide the Christmas cake? I feel like something rich and strange for dessert when I've attended to you," she said, as she set the tray down.

"I don't have one," Yannick said, surprised.

"Really? But you *make* Christmas cake. You're a baker, and you made some beautiful ones for the firm."

"Yes, but—" He tried to think how to explain why he didn't have a Christmas cake at *Langelhame*, but the impoverished state of his life had taken such a sharp turn the reasoning seemed far away.

"Next year, we shall have a Christmas cake," Chiara announced, tickling his balls. "We'll all take turns stirring."

"That's Christmas pudding," Lili said.

"Well, we'll have a pudding, too. And can we have another Langel *Liebeskuchen*?"

"I already have my heart's desire," he said.

"Yes, but we could have it anyway."

"We'll get more apples from Irish," Chiara said.

"And then we'll send them back to the firm in the marketing baskets—"

"And *you* will totally steal them."

Lili's eyes lit up with an unholy joy that sat oddly on her cherubic features. "Maybe . . ." Her voice sounded sinister and he stared at her.

"Maybe . . ." Now his Chiara was going sinister, too.

"Maybe," they said together . . .

"We'll catch you at it—"

"And then we'll—"

"Punish you."

"Like this!"

Chiara put both hands on his shoulders, pinning him to the bed.

Lili whisked around and grabbed his knees, forcing them down.

She bent slowly . . . slowly . . . positioned her lips and blew a loud, rude raspberry directly into his belly.

Chiara kissed him, and then she turned her head to look at her sister. "He *smiled*. He did. He totally *smiled*."

"Excellent." Lili handed each of them a cup and then she got back into bed.

Chiara sipped the tea gratefully, and then she glanced at Lili.

"*Schwester?*"

"Hm?"

"We totally eloped with the baker. Did you ever expect to elope with the baker?"

"I think I can safely say it never occurred to me."

Chiara said, "I wonder why not?" She focused on Yannick. "Did you ever expect to elope?"

"I never expected anything . . . I never hoped—" He broke

off, aware again that he would seem pathetic if he said more.

His lovelies homed in on his omission.

"Were we—"

"Did we—"

They stopped. Lili said, "Why were you so difficult to know?"

"Mistress Martina made it clear you two were out of my reach," he said.

"What?"

"No!"

"She's not like that."

"That's—"

"Ridiculous!"

Lili said, "You're so talented. You could work anywhere, even in the city."

"I need to be near the gates so I can come home between shifts."

"*Tante* thinks she's lucky to have you. She says bakers are a special breed."

"She certainly wouldn't think you weren't good for us."

"Why would you think that?"

He cast his mind back to the first weeks of his employment. "She gave me a little warning to keep my hands off you. She was kind about it, but I saw if I got out of line, I'd have to leave."

"That was *years* ago," Chiara said.

"She never rescinded the warning."

"Why would she? You never showed the slightest interest."

"He did though, by *not* showing it," Lili said.

"We're not her little nieces to be watched over now."

"We're grown up, and we can make our own choices."

"And we definitely made the right choice with you."

He relaxed as yet another complication unravelled and

drifted away.

The twins settled again, warm and flexible as cats.

"I'd like —"

He broke off, wondering what he'd been about to say.

Everything is fine.

Endorphins flooded through him and he relaxed into the bed.

"Mm?" Lili murmured.

"I'd like us to get priested . . . To be a family."

CHAPTER THIRTEEN: SWANS

Chiara, December Twenty-seventh

"What?"

Chiara felt the bedclothes shift as Lili sat up.

"What about *what?*" she asked, feeling confused. She had been floating on a warm sea of comfort.

"Yannick wants to get married," Lili said.

That was a big *what*, indeed. "Married? We—we can't."

This time Yannick sat up. He looked bewildered. "I thought—"

Chiara patted his shoulder. "We're here with you. This is home, you're ours and we're yours. We're family."

"But you won't be my wives."

"*Gott im Himmel!*" Lili exclaimed. She sounded like *Tante Martina*. "Tell him . . . explain . . ." She trailed off, and Chiara heard her take a big breath.

"She means we can't marry you," Chiara said. She saw his face stiffen and rushed on. "But *only* because you can't have two wives at the same time."

"You could marry one of us, and then we can still be a family," Lili said.

"I could never choose. I want you both."

Chiara exchanged a mystified look with Lili. How could Yannick not be aware that the law said one spouse was your lot?

"It's—"

Yannick said, "Do you know Hamish Almaclair?"

"No," Lili said.

Chiara corrected, "We don't *know* him, Lil, but we know about him. He runs the dance troupe that performed at the

68

festival back in April. You remember . . . that big braeman."

"Oh, yes . . . What about him?"

"Has he got two wives?" Chiara asked. She knew he couldn't have, though he was surely big enough and lively enough to keep two women happy.

"I thought he might be gay," Lili said.

"What? Never!"

"He runs the troupe with that hot courtfolk man *Tante* fancies. You know the one. He comes in for her special coffee."

Yannick said, "Master Almaclair doesn't have two wives. He and Gervais share the same one. Her name's Flori."

"How do you know?" Lili asked.

"I pass them at the gateway sometimes when they go to the McTavish bothy in the braelands. She's human."

"Well!"

"I suppose we might ask them how they swung it," Chiara said. She hadn't thought so far as marriage, but the idea was appealing. "We could make a new name and be Yannick, Lili and Chiara Langel-Bless," she said.

She lay down again, pulled Yannick down beside her, and kissed his neck. "You smell lovely." She rolled onto her back and gazed up at the ceiling. The sunlight dappled down on the big bed, and she stretched. The sky was clear, and she saw three black swans flying overhead, framed by the skylight.

"Oh, look!" She pointed, entranced by the graceful birds.

Yannick looked as if watching swans through the roof was an everyday matter. She supposed it was, to him.

Or maybe not so everyday . . . He stiffened.

She snapped around to see a look of horror come over his face.

"Yannick?" she faltered.

His face blanched.

Worried, she looked across at Lili for support. There was still so much they didn't know about *over here*, as well as about their newly acquired lover.

Lili shrugged her answer.

The swans had flown out of sight, but surely they couldn't be the problem. Since when were swans considered bad luck? Quite the opposite. Weren't they those faithful birds that paired up for life? Even better, this was a threesome.

"Yannick, what's wrong?" she asked.

Wordlessly, he indicated a clock on the wall. It was the old-fashioned type of pendulum clock, and Chiara hadn't noticed it before.

She stared at it uncomprehendingly for a few seconds before an explanation clicked in her mind.

It must have stopped at midnight.

With a soundless flick, the minute hand moved to overtake the hour.

It was after twelve o'clock.

It can't be!

She settled back against Yannick. "Looks as if I got my Christmas sleep-in after all."

Yannick said, "How could I have slept so long? I *never* oversleep."

Lili giggled. "Could be to do with having a reason to be relaxed. We totally wore you out."

"Mistress Martina will be furious with me."

Hm. There is that . . .

"She'll be furious with us, too," Chiara said. She knew that, intellectually, but she didn't seem to feel it. Eating charmed cake, wishing, eloping and being yodelled twice over by her delicious baker and then seeing three magical swans fly over seemed to have pushed an aunt—even a beloved aunt who was their employer—and her righteous anger a long way down her list of priorities. "She'll be okay. She can get the casuals in."

"You're taking it calmly." Yannick's colour was coming back. Maybe it had something to do with Lili rubbing his neck.

"There's no point it flying into a panic."

"What about the bread?"

"*Tante* can make *eierbrot*. You left the ingredients ready for her . . . remember?"

She remembered something else they'd left ready, and she gasped on a giggle. She and Lili had left a note in the egg bowl to surprise Yannick. By now it would have totally surprised *Tante* Martina.

She'll know what's happened. She won't be pleased, but she won't be worried either.

She patted Yannick's arm, appreciating the firm muscles. All that kneading and mixing must give him a brilliant daily workout. "Yannick, listen. *Tante* will be annoyed, but she will manage okay. She won't sack us, because if she did, that would complicate our lives, and our wish uncomplicated them. Besides, she'll find our message. Right, Lil?"

"Exactly." Lili nodded vigorously and convincingly, which pleased Chiara, as she was making it up as she went along.

"She loves us, and we love you. It will be—"

Ooh. I love him. I really-truly do.

"What message?" Yannick asked.

"We left one in the larder," Lili said. She didn't mention it hadn't been meant for *Tante* Martina.

"*Tante* will tell Mum and Dad and—"

"Mum will be furious."

"But with luck, the fuss will be over before we go back to the firm."

"We'd better go right now," Yannick said.

"No. We need to stay here." Chiara felt the certainty she had been only pretending before. "Three days, at least," she added.

"We decided we have to consolidate," Lili added.

"Because, after all, you're ours and we're yours, but it's new to us and so we need to be together for a while . . ."

"With no interruptions . . ."

"So we can sort out our new dynamics . . ."

"Which *totally* work." Chiara nodded to Lili and said, "Think of it as an early honeymoon."

Chapter Fourteen: Honeymoon

Yannick, December Twenty-seventh

Yannick knew his lovelies were playing him with twin-talk, but it was such a novelty to have love and attention focused on him that he dropped his objections. He knew he might have to pay for his pleasures later, whatever the twins said, but it was done now, and he felt ready to let things go.

They were right. Their elopement couldn't be undone, and he wouldn't have if he could.

She loves us and we love you. Chiara's voice sounded in his mind.

"What do people usually do on honeymoons?" he asked.

Chiara smiled at him and tickled his neck. "We've never had one before, so we get to choose what we want to do."

"I think we're meant to do you, Yannick," Lili said, straight-faced.

"And you're meant to do us," Chiara added.

"But we'll remember there's one of you to two of us, so you can always say *let's just cuddle*, or ask for a raincheck." Lili's words were reasonable, but she was tugging gently on his shoulders, turning him to face her. She was still wearing his red bed-shirt, but she'd untied the strings and her breasts swelled out, tempting his mouth. "I love having you suck me," she added.

That was plain enough.

Chiara kissed his cheek. "I think I'll go to the tub room. Is that what you called it? After that, I'll go outside for a bit and see what home looks like in daylight."

He noticed with pleasure that she wasn't asking permission. She was telling them what she planned to do. He moved

73

his face back from Lili's generous chest and aimed a kiss at his lovely Chiara. As she chose that moment to get out of bed, his lips caught her a glancing brush on her bottom. She made an extraordinary sound that he thought of as a coo of joy. "Ooh. Do that again."

Laughing, he did it again, much more thoroughly, and then he returned his face to Lili's bosom.

Lili wrapped her arms around him, and she held him tightly against her. Soon she was whimpering with pleasure as she straddled his cock.

"Don't forget the yelp," she said, between gasps.

He cried out.

"Yes, do it like that when it's time—"

"It *is* time!" he panted.

"Ooh—really?" She lifted away on her elbows, and he caught the flash of her smile. Her blue eyes were almost all dark so she must be—

She gasped in a breath and squealed, and he went with her before they collapsed in one another's arms.

"I'll—get—you a cloth."

She hugged him fiercely. "Later. It's lovely of you to do that, but for now, I want to just be here with you."

He was asleep before he knew it.

By the time he woke again, it was three o'clock and he was alone in the bed.

He should have made the scones by now, but he pushed the thought away.

A note rested on the pillow beside him and he picked it up. *Just Eloped,* it said. The two words were enclosed in a heart.

He went to the tub room and cleaned up, making a point to conjure fresh sheets on to the bed. This *Just Eloped* stuff was messy.

He dressed in what he thought of as *proper clothes,* and he went to find his lovelies.

They were in the kitchen, examining the stores. Lili was still wearing his red bed-shirt, and Chiara had helped herself to a blue one. They'd fed the stove, and the kettle was hissing softly.

He held out his arms, and they abandoned the pantry to kiss him.

"We're having a picnic for dinner," Chiara said, into his neck.

"We wanted to know . . ."

"Where your favourite picnic place is."

"There's Langeltarn, over on the alpen meadow," he said, although picnics hadn't been on his agenda for years.

"Can we go there in these shirts?"

"Or will people look at us funny?"

He said, cautiously, "You look adorable, but it wouldn't be considered *usual*." He wondered how much they knew of the dress code and how widely it differed among the various orders of the fay. Did *living human* as they had mean they'd be shocked if they met a water lad in all his naked glory? What about a tree maid who might be half-wearing a sarong?

I'll have to give them a crash course in how to react and in what not to say . . .

He smiled to himself. No. They always reacted naturally and kindly, and he wouldn't change that for the world.

If they happened to tell a water lad he had a pretty cock, then the water lad would be pleased that they had noticed.

"Dirndls, then," they decided.

He saw they'd assembled bread and cheese, gingerbread and some dried cherries, so he fetched some beer from the cellar to go with it.

"Do you drink beer?" he asked, belatedly.

"As long as it's not peach schnapps—"

"Mixed with poteen—"

"We drink anything."

"Only not denatured coffee," Lili added.

"That's just *wrong.*"

"You won't find coffee *over here* at all," he said absently. He noted Chiara was staring at him. "What is it, lovely?"

"Are these *lederhosen?*" she asked, looking sideways at Lili. "They are, aren't they?"

"They totally are—"

"They're *lederhosen.*"

"Our baker wears *lederhosen.*"

"These are *kniebundhosen.* Knee breeches," he said, puzzled by their hilarity.

"They make your bum look *great,*" Lili said. She walked around him, smiling. "Yannick, do cameras work *over here?*"

"Ye-es."

"You don't sound too certain."

"Electronic ones don't. Some of the older film cameras do, but mostly people have paintings, like the ones Master Peckerdale did for the café, only miniature. Why do you ask?"

Lili said, "It would be nice to have a photo record of our honeymoon."

"We'll find someone who has a camera," he said, although he knew it would be difficult. "There's a leprechaun man wed to a pixie—he's Master Peckerdale's brother, and they live over at KerryKenny. I believe he uses one sometimes."

"It would be nice, but never mind that now." Chiara conjured the collected food into a small basket Yannick used for berry picking and then pushed the kettle back from the hob. "I'm guessing you don't have vacuum flasks?"

"No, but we can conjure tea things to the tarn. There's a flat rock there that folk use for cooking."

"Excellent! How do we get there?"

"Just the same as we got here. We just hold hands and *go.*"

They ate their picnic at the tarn, and then they swam, which was something Yannick hadn't had the leisure to do for a long time.

The lovelies gasped and shivered in the bracing water, so he conjured blankets to wrap around them when they were dry. The curious *alpenziegan* came bleating up to sniff and nudge.

"I'll milk one of the does tomorrow," he said, watching his twins sitting shoulder-deep in a rabble of multi-hued creatures.

"It'd be good to sleep here one night," Chiara said, laughing as soft noses poked in the folds of her blanket, looking for gingerbread. "Not tonight, though, maybe we could leave it for a few weeks until it's warmer."

"It will be warm enough now. I have plenty of wool blankets."

"You *do*?"

"Yes. Made from *alpenziegan* wool." He laughed at their expressions. "This is the *Langelhame* flock. Didn't you know?"

They shook their heads.

"Besides, I'll keep you both warm," he said.

They packed up and returned to *Langelhame* where they drank more tea, explored the small, productive garden, and then retired up the stairs to their bed.

Yannick wanted to stay awake to enjoy his newfound life of warmth and affection, but after a far too brief stargazing session, he fell asleep.

CHAPTER FIFTEEN: WEDDING RINGS

Yannick, December Twenty-eighth

Yannick woke in the early hours with pins and needles in his left hand and a face-full of long hair.

He wiggled his fingers hopefully and blew the hair out of his mouth. The twin to his left purred as his fingers encountered her thigh and the one on his right sighed and turned over. She pressed her nose against his neck, breathing in before giving his ear a sleepy nip.

My Lili.

It was probably close to three o'clock, and he should have been on the pathway to the gate, ready to drive the short distance to *Fee Kaffee* and then let himself into the darkened kitchen to wake the stove.

Instead, he was lying in cosy and delighted discomfort, with one twin whispering a hopeful suggestion in his ear.

He rolled gently to the right, capturing a willing mouth.

From the left, an arm slid around his waist and gave him a playful tickle.

"Mm?"

"I'll have what she's having, but later," Chiara said. She kissed the back of his neck, patted his bum and then rolled over and curled so her buttocks nestled in the small of his back.

Half an hour later, Lili was sleeping again, so he rolled and gathered her twin against him, kissing her forehead gently.

"I'm not asleep," she said, and she kissed him back before she murmured, "I like having my back rubbed."

"Me, too," he whispered.

"Me three," Lili said from behind him.

In the morning, the twins found alphorns stored in the rock-cut cellar, and they speculated on who might have played them.

Yannick didn't know, but he showed them his flugelhorn and his flute, and he discovered, with mild astonishment, that they didn't know how to play.

Music was second nature *over here*. How could his lovelies not know how to finger a flute?

"We'll soon learn proper fingering," they assured him, but from the angle of Chiara's gaze, he wondered if a flute was what she really had in mind.

They walked hand in hand through the valley called *Helles Tal*, and then they went to Treborrow, where Tane Pendennis, the halfling jeweller, agreed to make them rings.

"Forever wedding rings or just-for-nows?" he asked.

Yannick saw Tane noticing the twins, who were obviously noticing him. Maybe they hadn't seen a man in a pisky kilt before.

Tane's father was a pisky man, but his mother was a water maid, so he might just as well have been working his craft in a state of nature.

Remembering his resolve to let his lovelies react in their instinctive ways, Yannick hadn't said anything to prepare them for this.

Lili caught his eye and grinned, waggling her eyebrows. "He's a bit mature, but totally hot," she murmured.

Yannick glanced at the jeweller, who laughed and nodded his agreement of the description.

"I'd be happy to play with you, my maids, but—" He glanced at his wife, a fair-haired scatterblood called Jillian, who was turning the pages of a book for their youngest child.

"Don't mind me, sweetheart," she said, waving a hand.

Tane raised an eyebrow at Yannick, possibly asking

permission.

Yannick shrugged and turned out his hands.

"It's up to my lovelies what they do and who they choose to do it with."

The halfling turned the full force of his personality on the twins.

"Want to play with me, then, *mädchens*?" he asked.

Lili and Chiara looked nonplussed for a second and then smiled back.

Chiara called to Yannick, "What does he mean? I bet it isn't *Scrabble*."

Jillian said, "He means the loud and happy kind of play, dear. In water or on land, swinging from the trees, or bouncing about in a bed. My man is endlessly horny and endlessly adaptable. He knows exactly how to give you the best time of your life."

Tane blew her a kiss. "I'm not so adaptable as you, my darling Jillian Jules."

"Oh." The twins appeared to consult between themselves, and then they turned back to the jeweller.

"Thanks, but . . ."

"No, because . . ."

"We have our own Yannick . . ."

"To love, and he keeps us busy."

Lili gave her naughtiest smile. "And we keep *him* busy, don't we, Yannick?"

"Very," he said. "Lots of yodelling," he added, somewhat aghast at himself.

The jeweller laughed, setting his many silver charms chiming. "Lucky man, but your cock might require some butter after a few nights with this pair," he said.

"Butter?" Lili enquired.

"Old leppy remedy, dear, or so I hear. Never had to use it myself," Jillian said.

"Wedding forever rings or just-for-nows?" Tane Pendennis repeated, returning to business.

Yannick waited to see if his lovelies would raise more objections about legality, or if they'd choose to enquire further into the uses of butter. To his pleasure, they chorused, "Wedding forever."

Lily came and leaned on him. "We'll get the rings and sort out the logistics later," she said.

"Do you need to get our ring sizes or anything?" Chiara asked the jeweller.

"No . . . these will fit the people they're meant for. Did you have a design in mind, or shall I just let the love take me where it will?"

"Shall we leave it to Master Pendennis?" Yannick suggested to the twins.

They nodded eagerly.

"What can we offer you in exchange?" he asked, as was the custom. He knew Tane Pendennis used money in the human realm, but this was *over here.*

Jillian answered, "We both like cake, Master Langel. What about something special from your great-grandmother's mysterious book?"

"You could make them Langel *Liebeskuchen*," Lili suggested helpfully.

"No, lovely. Christmas is over, and now that's only ever for us." He turned to Jillian. "Butter *Erdbeerkuchen* is a good one, and I have never made it for anyone but my grandmother. It was her favourite."

"Oh?"

"Butter strawberry cake," he translated.

"That sounds perfect."

And so the deal was struck.

An hour later, they had three matching wedding rings incised with triple hearts.

To make the exchange, they had to pick alpine strawberries, milk the *alpenziegen*, make butter and begin the baking.

After that, they needed to work on those logistics of getting priested.

First though . . .

Yannick offered his hands to his lovelies. "What would you like to do before we get that baking begun?"

"Go home and explore," they said together.

From the identical laughing looks they bestowed on him he knew the *exploring* was going to involve getting him out of his britches.

Chapter Sixteen: The Priesting Solution

Lili, December Thirtieth

Lili had certainly not expected to elope with a baker, find a new home and get married in the space between Christmas and New Year.

Nevertheless, that was what was happening for her and Chiara.

Getting priested was the way Yannick chose to put it.

"I never knew he had so many different ways to think of things," Lili said to Chiara as they took it in turns to work the butter churn. She had also thought goats' milk couldn't be made into butter, but apparently, *alpenziegen* weren't exactly goats and their milk did set cream.

"We never knew because he never talked to us," Chiara pointed out.

It was odd to reflect that until Saint Stephen's Day they'd never really known his voice. Now, it was as dear and familiar to Lili as Chiara's.

Lili heard the subtle sound as the cream *turned,* and together, she and her sister sorted out how to convert the yellow lumps into proper butter.

They knew they could leave it for Yannick, but, having discussed the matter over his beloved sleeping form when they'd tired him out in bed, they'd opted for *total immersion* in all things *over here.*

"Just because we've always *lived human,* it doesn't mean we can't learn to be proper *mädchens,*" Chiara said.

They'd expected Yannick to arrange some sort of liaison with the Almaclairs to work things out, but the priesting solution came from a totally unexpected source.

They were still working on the butter in the kitchen when someone knocked on the outer door.

What?

It couldn't be Yannick. He was out gathering strawberries, and he certainly wouldn't knock on their own door.

"I suppose . . ." Lili said.

"We'd better answer that."

"What if it's that uncle?"

"We'll offer him tea or beer."

"It might be the jeweller . . ."

"Or Jillian. I liked her."

"Got to be thirty or so but she's . . ."

"Hot."

They abandoned the butter and conjured the door open.

"Hello? Greet you?"

The voice was vaguely familiar.

"Oh, shit-shit-shit . . . do we just walk in, or what?"

"Come on in," Lili called.

They heard footsteps and the hanging swung aside to reveal Tab Merriweather, hand in hand with Josefa.

The four of them stared, each pair equally disconcerted to see the other two.

"Unbelievable!" Tab said.

Josefa, a tall, gangling young woman with black hair, broke into a charming three-cornered grin. "The plot thickens . . . You're the *Fee Kaffees*, right?"

"Lili and Chiara. They're Martina's nieces," Tab clarified. He frowned. "I didn't expect to see you two here."

"Why not?"

"We live here."

He flung up his hands. "Don't go all x-ray predator twinnish on me, you mad *mädchens*. Do you happen to know where Yannick Lengel is?"

"He's picking strawberries on an alp," Lili said, seeing no

reason not to tell him.

"Strawberries?" Josefa's eyes lit up.

"Yes . . . why do you want him?"

"That's his business."

Josefa elbowed her betrothed in the ribs. "It's their business, too, I reckon." She turned her attention back to the twins. "So—you found someone to give yourselves to for Christmas?"

"He's keeping us forever," Chiara said.

"We told you we'd make nice presents."

"That was quick work. Can I tell my brothers they're safe from your machinations?"

Josefa gave Tab the elbow again. "Get on with it, Tab. I have to be back at work in less than an hour and I'm going to be late as it is."

Tab said, "Okay . . . look, I'll conjure a note to Tan to come and get you. If you start walking, he'll meet you at the head of the valley."

Josefa nodded and kissed him. "See you tonight, then." She smiled at the twins and went out to meet Tab's next brother down, who was presumably going to pilot her back through the gate. Josefa was human, and so she wouldn't be able to open the gate for herself.

"Just a mo—" Tab conjured a notepad and scribbled a message to his brother before dismissing it. "Okay. Now, the reason I'm here is that Peck sent me."

Peck?

He must have seen their bewilderment because he said, "You know Grene's Motor Clinic?"

"Yes, near the tower," Lili said.

"Right. Peck Grene—he's Mum's cousin—runs it. He's a scary pixie man, but he's been less scary since he married Chloe—Chloe is Josefa's bestie. With me so far?"

"No. Aren't *you* Josefa's bestie?"

"Yes, but Josefa says she can easily manage two."

"Is Peck your bestie, too?"

"No, he's my mum's cousin and a scary pixie man . . . look, never mind. Just focus on the garage, okay?"

"Okay."

"The garage is outside the Peckerdale-Grene wards because if it weren't, cars wouldn't work there. So Peck fixes up cars for people. He growls at the owners for neglecting their gearsticks. He always growls at Josefa over what she does to her ute."

"What's he going on about now, Lil?" Chiara asked.

Lili shrugged. They'd learned not to discuss Yannick when he was present and awake, but they didn't see why Tab should get the same courtesy.

"Don't *do* that," Tab complained.

"Um?"

"God, you *mädchens* are mad. Anyway, aside from fixing cars, Peck lets folk park their vehicles in the side lot when they use the gate in the copse. We leave the ute and my van there every night, and Hamish and Gervy park there—oh, lots of folk. It saves them parking on the roadside, which would look peculiar to humans who don't know about the gate.

"One of the people who parks there is Yannick Langel. Peck grabbed Josefa and me this morning and said Yannick's van had been parked there since Boxing Day and that wasn't normal."

"Why would he care?" Lili asked.

"He doesn't care. Only he's got this fix-it thing. I mean, he's a cranky git, but if he thinks something's wrong, he gets an urge to make it better. So he got this manic pixie gleam in his eyes and latched on to Josefa and me and asked us to hunt up Yannick and see if he's okay."

"He's quite okay," Lili said. She smiled, thinking of just how wonderfully *okay* Yannick had been when they finally left their bed that morning.

"Why *you* though?" Chiara asked.

Tab looked surprised. "Josefa and I live here. We've got a cabin down in the alpen meadow. Didn't you know?"

"No . . . why would we?"

"Why would you. Come to that. I don't know where *you* live. At the café with Martina?"

"No, we live *here*," Lili reminded.

"We used to live in Dodge—"

"But we have totally managed to *get out of Dodge*."

Tab threw up his hands. "Okaaay. Don't go mad-*mädchen* on me. But do me a favour, aye, and get Yannick to go and tell Peck he's okay. Otherwise, Peck will be on my case, and I don't have time to defuse a manic pixie on a twice-daily basis. I have—how did you put it? A cock to stick where the sun don't shine and a woman to impress with my prowess and maturity." He shook his head. "Unbelievable!"

"We'll tell him," Lili said. She trusted Yannick would understand whatever all that was about.

Chiara said, "Tab, do you know how we can get priested?"

"No. Let me know if you find out. I've been trying to get priested with Josefa, like, forever." He laughed at their expressions. "Actually, I know two fay priests, which is what I assume you want. Rory Inkersoll is a grand old git—he's the one who married Peck to his Chloe. But just now I think he's sailing with his dad . . . um . . . I reckon your best bet is Father Dai Daffyd. He's a teg, and he'll likely sing at you . . . but if you don't mind having an operatic teg singing your service, he'll be your man. Want me to get him to call on you here, later today?"

"Yes, please," Lili said.

"Grand. If you get priested tonight after work, Josefa will be back, and we can be your *siaradwyr cariad*." He pronounced the term with care.

"Our what?"

"Love speakers. Kind of like witnesses. It's a teg thing." He brightened. "If I can get Josefa into a romantic mood, maybe she'll let Dai priest us, too!"

He looked at them for a few more seconds and smiled with surprising sweetness. "Felicitations, mad *mädchens*. I expect you'll be very happy. Be sure you make Yannick happy, too, okay?"

CHAPTER SEVENTEEN: PRIESTED

Chiara, December Thirtieth

The priest, Dai Daffyd, was a dark-eyed teg man from the valleys.

He arrived at *Langelhame* at seven o'clock, and he apologised for the delay.

"I had to commune with my soul to see my way in this," he said in his musical accent.

"Your way to marrying two of us to one of Yannick?" Chiara asked.

The young priest nodded. "Yes, but then I thought of what Father Rory would say. It goes along the lines of *Do the kindest thing.* It seems to me the kindest thing is to not trouble my bishop with this matter. He is a very good man and a very busy man. It would not be kind of me to disturb him." He was setting up his accoutrements as he spoke.

"There is no set form for a threesome wedding, so we'll wing it. First off, are you three truly committed to one another? If not, I can't in all conscience perform this wedding."

Yannick squeezed Chiara's hand.

"Yes, we are," they all said.

"Sharing one man might not always come easily . . ." the priest said.

Chiara laughed. "Oh, it does, though. Sharing is what Lili and I have always done. We totally share loving Yannick, and he shares love with us."

"He has one mouth, but he also has—" Lili's voice subsided into a mumble as Josefa gagged her with her hand.

Tab coughed and said, "Man, don't ask about that. It'll only make you blush."

"I think you should shift your hand," Yannick said to Josefa. "Lili sometimes bites."

"Eek!" Josefa snatched her hand away.

"If you're ready, we can proceed." Dai Daffyd called them gently to order.

Holding hands with Yannick, and aware of Tab Merriweather at her elbow, Chiara held her breath. She realised, with a qualm, that she was waiting for the priest to ask Yannick if he took Lili before turning his attention to her.

I won't mind. We share.

She listened to the wedding service, although it wasn't quite the one she remembered hearing when one of Nina's sisters married a barrister.

For one thing, the priest was singing in an operatic tenor.

Here it came . . .

"Do you, Yannick, take —" Incredibly, he paused.

Yannick squeezed her hand reassuringly and responded, "I, Yannick, take these lovelies to be my forever wives . . . to love and to share all that I have and all that I am."

Chiara felt tears running down her cheeks, and the priest turned his dark, compassionate gaze on her.

"Do you, the lovelies, take this man to love and to share for as long as you three shall live?"

"We do," she blurted.

Tears dripped down her dirndl and she heard someone sob behind her.

Josefa ran around and pressed a handkerchief into her hand. "Mop up, sweetie. You're making my Tab cry and he has to be able to make the response."

Chiara wiped her face, and Yannick turned to hug her, with Lili's arm coming around her, too.

The priest said gently, "Kneel, my children, and make sure you're close. I need to span three heads for the benediction."

They kneeled together and were blessed by the singing priest.

Finally, he stepped back and said, "Tabor and Josefa, I now call on you to stand as *siaradwyr cariad*. Come and stand by me."

Chiara sniffled as Tab, somewhat red-eyed and sniffling just as much as Chiara, stood with Josefa facing them.

"Do you two see true love before you tonight?" the priest enquired.

Josefa leaned into Tab and whispered, "Speak up."

He jumped and said, "I do."

"And I do, too," Josefa said.

Dai Daffyd nodded approval, and then he said, "Yannick, you may kiss your brides."

Chiara recovered herself at last. Warmly tucked under Yannick's arm, she turned to see Josefa still comforting Tab.

"What's wrong—"

"With him?" Lili finished.

Josefa looked up at them in exasperation. "He's trying to guilt me into marrying him. Again."

"Why don't you then? He obviously loves you, and you love him," Chiara pointed out.

"Because I'm four years older and we agreed to wait . . . oh, stuff it." She stood back and poked Tab in the belly. "Stop that. I'm absolutely *not* going to marry a cry baby."

She turned to the priest. "Father Daffyd, have you got enough stamina left to tie me to him? He's not usually like this. I'm kind of a Catholic, but you have a *many rooms* service, right?"

At the priest's smiling nod, she said, "Shit-shit-shit . . . we need witnesses. It ought to be your brothers and Chloe, Tab, but we seem to have these three already here." She added, to Chiara, "His mum's going to be cross about missing the wedding, but we can do it all over again, sometime, and have a big party. You three are invited."

She turned to Tab, who was staring at her with his eyes a

sudden glow of opal. "Give me the camera, Tab. I'll snap a few pics for these lovely people, and then they can do the same for us."

Chapter Eighteen: The Reckoning

Lili, December Thirty-first

Lili found the night after their impromptu wedding unexpectedly quiet.

There was something about being married that made her feel the need for calm.

"Chiara and I need to sort things out with *Tante*," she said to Yannick as they dried themselves after a tub.

"*We* need to sort them out," he said.

"Yes, we do, but I think she and I have to do it first. I hope you understand."

Yannick conjured the towel over to the fire rack to dry. "I do. You're her family."

"So are you now."

"She doesn't know that yet. Come to bed, lovelies. It's too late for a three o'clock start, but we need to go back in the morning. I'll stop by Master Peckerdale on the way."

Lili sighed. "If we're going to have you for our wedding night, we'd better get cracking," she said.

"Both together again, to save on time," Chiara suggested.

"Or maybe we could just cuddle. That's good, too."

"It's all good," Chiara said.

An hour later, Lili lay in her now-accustomed place tucked in her husband's right arm. She wanted to make the lovely quiet last longer, but much too soon, she was asleep.

Lili woke to find the bed empty, aside from herself. She went to wash, and she examined her face in the polished pierglass.

"Mistress Elizabeth Langel-Bless," she said aloud. Her full

first name usually meant her mother was delivering disapproval, but she quite saw it might come in useful one day if she wanted to be imposing.

She wondered if she and Chiara would need to change their names on their drivers' licences. The priest had assured them their wedding lines were real . . . but he'd also suggested they might be best kept private in the human realm.

"Weddings *over there* are a matter of law and precedent, rooted by custom in possession and dynasty," he'd explained gently. He'd smiled and added, "*Over here*, they're a matter for hearts and souls and the comfort of bed company."

Lili considered that a lovely way to put it. She wondered if the priest had *the comfort of bed company.* She hoped he did.

Yannick and Chiara were having breakfast, and Lili hurried to catch up.

"I didn't wake when you did," she said to Chiara.

"Maybe it's the new dynamic?" her twin said.

"Could be." Lili quickly ate while Chiara banked the fire in the stove.

"We'd better go, lovelies," Yannick said. Hand in hand, they left *Langelhame*, walked down Nordalp and stepped through the gate into the copse.

It was still quite early, and no one was about as they crossed the green belt and came up to Grene's Motor Clinic.

Yannick unlocked the van. "Hop in the back, lovelies," he said.

"You're kidnapping us?" Chiara sounded hopeful.

"No, I'm storing you safely, so you don't go wandering off while I go and talk to Master Grene."

He walked across the short strip of gravel and vanished into the garage.

Lili watched him go, thinking wistfully of the day before which had been made of knee breeches, butter, a singing priest, a tearful witness and two surprising weddings. "Do you think he's going to revert to grumpy-baker-mode?" she asked.

She jumped as a loud ping sounded from her pocket.

Message.

She ignored it.

Chiara shook her head. "Not a chance. He looks like the old Yannick dressed like that, but we know better."

Lili thought of their husband kneeling over them in their bed and kissing them in turn and then holding them tightly against him. Her stomach felt as if it was liquifying. "He's so—"

Ping! Ping! Ping!

Chiara's phone had joined in now.

"Dammit!" Lili conjured hers out of her pocket and glanced at the screen. "Mum, Mum, *Tante*, Mum, *Tante* . . . Ugh, I can't do this now." She switched off the phone and dumped it on the seat.

Chiara did the same with hers, not even glancing at the fusillade of texts.

Silence.

Chiara took Lili's hand and continued her train of thought. "He is *so*. Exactly. He loves us and he needs us."

"That's not about being needy though . . ."

"No, I shouldn't think so. How long is it since someone gave him any love, do you think? Aside from us?"

"I suppose his old granny loved him. And Missus Palmer seems to have been kind. I hope we get to meet her and thank her for that."

"*Tante* has been *kind* to him, I expect, but it's not the same, is it?"

"It's not the same," Lili agreed soberly.

"Lucky he has us to love him forever," Chiara said.

They sat holding hands, silenced by the enormity of it.

"All those texts! Mum's going to be so furious," Chiara said at last.

"Hm."

"I wonder if she'll forgive us . . ."

Lili shrugged. "I don't know. I hope she will, but she hasn't been pleased with us for a long time now. I don't think there was anything we could have done about that, either."

"We could have gone to uni and got *useful* degrees. That would have pleased her."

"We could have, I suppose. But what if we'd pressed *her* to work in a café, or to throw pots?"

"Also in a café?"

"No, *Dummkopf!* On a potter's wheel. Would she have done that to please *us*?"

"No, but we'd never ask her to. She loves her job."

"And we love ours."

"She sees what she and Dad do as *worthwhile.*"

"What we do is worthwhile. We brighten up the place."

"We certainly brightened up Yannick," Chiara said.

Yannick came back, stuck his head into the van and smiled. "Master Peckerdale has simmered down, and he asked me to felicitate you. He said he's been married for two years now, and he recommends it. He also added that his wife recommends it—just in case I thought he was the only appreciative one."

He got in and drove the short distance to *Fee Kaffee,* where he conjured open the garage and parked in his accustomed place.

Tante Martina's little hatch was in its usual spot, but that meant nothing, since she lived in a cottage connected to the firm.

They entered via the garage door.

Yannick hugged them. "Call me if you need me, lovelies."

"To save us from our big, bad aunt?" Chiara asked.

"For anything. Any time."

"Even if your dough is at a critical stage?"

He hesitated. "Well—"

"We'll be fine," Lili said. She tried to sound assured. Lili Bless might be apprehensive. Mistress Elizabeth Langel-Bless could surely do better.

Yannick kissed them, and then he went into the larder, where they heard him assembling ingredients.

The twins quietly set about readying the café.

It felt surreal.

It was so much like a normal morning, except that it wasn't really a bit like that. They should have been at the market, and Yannick should have had the baking well underway.

"Where's *Tante*?" Lili wondered aloud as she laid the first tables. She glanced at the connecting door to the cottage.

"Marketing," Chiara said, coming out with the chalkboard. "Yannick said the market baskets just turned up. I'll go and unpack them."

Lili laid the second row of tables.

"Lil, come and see this!" Chiara called from the larder.

She went to look, glancing at Yannick, who was cracking large eggs into a basin. She leaned up to kiss his cheek, and he smiled.

"Look!" Chiara had the baskets half unpacked.

Lili looked, frowning. "That's just the marketing." She saw tomatoes and strawberries and a couple of summer melons. The strawberries looked large and pale after the alpine berries they'd been eating at *Langelhame*.

"Since when does *Tante* buy *these*?" Chiara held up hand-made chocolates and a box of dried orange slices dusted with powdered sugar. Next came a selection of speciality cheeses, some tiny imported toasts and spiced ham.

"Maybe she's having a party?" Lili suggested.

"Not enough for that."

"It's New Year's Eve, so maybe she's going to one?"

"Could be, but what *I* think is that she's found a courtfolk man to play with."

"She hasn't done that lately . . . as far as I know. I thought she had her eye on that singer back in April . . ." Lili shrugged and abandoned speculation. She glanced at the door. The appearance of those baskets meant a vanishingly small window of time before *Tante* came back and they had to face the reckoning.

She hoped the casuals would hurry up and come in. *Tante* wouldn't want to cause a scene in front of them.

She went out to the garden to pick some flowers for the tables and stopped to stare at a scattering of white feathers on the grass.

How odd.

She carried the flowers inside and arranged them.

The door opened, and *Tante* Martina came in with her light step. She was smiling to herself, but the smile fell off when she spotted Lili.

"*Guten morgen,* Tante," Lili ventured.

Martina stared with her finely arched eyebrows rising.

Chiara peeped out of the kitchen. "*Kaffee?*"

Their aunt's grey eyes snapped sideways.

"Well, you've come back," she said coolly.

Lili nodded. "Yes. We've nearly finished setting up."

"*Kaffee?*" Chiara said again.

"I can get my own, thank you." Her gaze flicked between the twins. "I'm glad to see you two are intact."

"Um?"

"Not grievously injured, or lying in a hospital bed recovering from amnesia, or possibly carried off by marauding aliens."

"No, we're fine," Lili said.

Her stomach felt cold. This was worse than she'd expected.

"Have you contacted your mother?"

Lili shook her head.

"Hm. Do you happen to know where Yannick is?"

"He's in the larder, making a cherry cake," Chiara said. She glanced about. "When are the casuals coming in?"

"You mean Jen, Gretta and Angela?"

"Yes . . . we expected they'd be here by now."

Tante Martina looked at her grimly. "You might or possibly might not recall that Jen was going on a family holiday to Canberra. Gretta has her mother staying from Norway, so they're on a driving trip to Cape York. Angela . . . I'm unsure, but she is getting married tomorrow and is definitely not available. Why should she be? She had the week before her wedding off to prepare."

Lili cringed. *Tante* Martina sounded every bit as cutting as their mother.

"Fortunately, I *have* had some help," Martina said. Her face brightened.

"Oh, *good*. I do hope—"

"I wouldn't say he was quite as quick as you, but that's because there is just one of him and he doesn't conjure. He certainly made up for that with enthusiasm and dedication and, most importantly, with his *presence*."

The twins exchanged puzzled looks. Martina wasn't in the habit of hiring male casuals.

"He'll be here very soon to start his shift," Martina went on.

"Do we know him?" Chiara asked.

"No." Martina frowned slightly, and then she shifted to another subject. "I'm not asking where you've been," she said.

"Oh, we were—"

Their aunt's hand snapped up. "I don't need to know. I probably don't even want to know. Where you go and what you do outside work hours is not my business. As I told your parents when they persisted in annoying me, I am not your keeper. As your aunt, I have been concerned about you. I had to assume you were all right since there was no evidence to the contrary. I'm glad to see this is the case. However, as your employer, and as Yannick's employer, I do feel I am owed an explanation for your lack of consideration for your jobs."

Lili looked down at her toes.

"We left you a message," Chiara ventured.

"No, Chiara. A doodle on a napkin is not a message. A phone call is a message. An email or a text will do at a pinch. A note conjured to the café or to my cottage—that is a message. I couldn't send you one as I didn't know where to send it, but you undoubtedly knew how to contact me."

Lili felt chastened. She ventured to look up and saw the crinkle still between Martina's brows.

"If Dequan hadn't stepped up, I would have been in considerable trouble. The holiday season is *not* the time for recruiting new staff in a hurry."

"Dequan?" Chiara questioned.

"Dequan Qin. He came in for a coffee, and seeing me so shorthanded, he stepped into the kitchen and he started washing up. He's been helping out ever since, and when he comes in, you will behave yourselves."

They nodded and then Chiara said, "If you want to have a private lunch with him in the cottage, we can look after the firm."

"Why should you think I wanted that?" Martina sounded cool, but Lili spotted a small flush of pink on her cheeks. And *was* that a tiny mark just below her ear?

"There were some nice things in the marketing baskets, so I thought maybe you had someone coming for lunch," Chiara said.

"I did some personal shopping while I was at the market, yes. I haven't exactly had time for shopping over the past few days. Now, both of you go and finish setting up."

Martina headed for the kitchen and Chiara hastily stepped into the café just before the door could close on her dirndl.

Lili sighed, and Chiara puffed out her cheeks expressively.

"She's cross, all right," Lili said.

"I suppose she has a right to be. Is she sacking cross?"

"Possibly. It sounds as if this Dequan has made a good impression."

"We'll be okay if she sacks us. So will Yannick."

"Ye-es, but it will—I mean, it's totally our fault."

"Do you think it will help if we grovel?"

"Apologise, you mean?" Lili asked.

"Yes."

"Obviously, we need to do that, but it has to be *sorry we let you down*, not *sorry we eloped*."

"No—"

"Because we totally were right to elope."

"And we *had* to consolidate . . ." Chiara clarified.

"What about this Dequan, though? Do you think he's a courtfolk man? It's not a courtfolk name."

"Helping out in the kitchen isn't a very *court* thing to do."

"No-o, unless he wanted to get into her pants."

"That's odd since Yannick never wanted to get into *our* pants."

Lili giggled, feeling suddenly better. "No, you're right. He's more interested in having us out of our pants."

Chiara sighed happily. "To be fair, we like him out of his, too."

"Whatever happens, we get to go home to *Langelhame* tonight," Lili said.

Someone tapped urgently on the café door, and Lili conjured it open.

A man stepped inside as something—a car horn, maybe—honked out in the street. He snapped the door shut behind him with one hand as he swung a holdall in the other.

"My escort's back. I wonder if we should try yodelling them away again," he said as he headed for the kitchen door.

"Yodelling?" Lili asked Chiara.

The man laughed, tucking something into his holdall. "Well, it worked that first night when we put on the show for —"

He broke off suddenly and looked up.

His eyes widened as he saw Lili and Chiara.

For a few seconds, they regarded one another uneasily, and then he cleared his throat and smiled.

It was a charming smile.

He wasn't a courtfolk man, after all. Lili wasn't sure what he was. He could have been human, but he had an unusually contoured face and light brown hair.

He looked about *Tante* Martina's age, and Lili was sure she had never seen him before. She would have remembered.

His smile widened and he said, "Lili and Chiara, I assume."

Lili smiled back. "I'm Lili," she said.

"That makes me Chiara, and everyone says Lili first, which is odd since I come first alphabetically."

Chiara was clearly rattled, but Lili responded automatically, "I'm older, that's why."

"Ten minutes."

"A day, technically. Anyway," Lili said. Their old argument slipped along on its well-rehearsed tracks and petered out.

"You must be Dequan," Chiara said, after another little silence.

He went on smiling, and Lili quite saw why *Tante* Martina would want to enjoy a private lunch with him. Probably a private supper and a private breakfast, too.

He looked lovely but too fair and too — well, he didn't look like their Yannick.

"You've been helping *Tante* Martina and she says you're almost as useful as we are —" she said.

"And the *almost* is only because there's just one of you," Chiara said, catching on.

"And of course we can greet you properly—"

"Because if you've been yodelling *Tante* Martina—"

Lili almost choked at that, but he *had* mentioned it first, so she carried on gamely. "You must be special—"

"But we can't try you out because—"

"You see, we're—"

"Off the menu," they said together.

Lili wanted to explode into laughter at his bemused expression, but there was still a gleam of humour in his eyes. He looked like fun.

"Stop that."

Oops. *Tante* Martina had come out of the kitchen. Her voice was curt, but her face softened into a sweet smile.

The man turned to her as if drawn by a magnet and smiled back.

Lili saw how pleased they were with one another and she relaxed. With Dequan to distract her, *Tante* would soon be back in a good humour. With luck, the worst of the reckoning was over.

Chapter Nineteen: Takk Engel

Chiara, December Thirty-first

Chiara saw Lili relax and she thought the worst was probably over.

Tante Martina turned to them, and Chiara waited for a smile of forgiveness. She knew they'd need to apologise, but for now, things should go back to normal.

Martina's eyes, softly smiling at her man, turned flinty as she looked at the twins.

She flicked her fingers dismissively.

Chiara saw Lili looking like a deer in the headlights and took her by the arm. "Come on . . ."

Lili jumped.

Martina stared them down. "Go and help Yannick, girls. I'll deal with you later."

"Yes, *Tante*," they said together.

Chiara tugged Lili towards the larder.

Yannick turned to them immediately. He had batter splashes up his arms, and he conjured a cloth and wiped himself down. "Come here, lovelies . . ."

Chiara pushed her face into his shoulder. She heard a small sob from Lili.

"What did Mistress Martina say to you?" he asked.

Chiara said, "What we expected. She's cross, but —"

"A man's been helping her. His name's Dequan."

"He's kind of hot," Chiara said.

"But not the way you are." Lili snuggled closer.

"I *wish* we were at home. Then we could all get into bed and cuddle until we feel better," Chiara said mournfully.

"We'll be back home tonight," Yannick said. He lifted his

head. "That is unless you lovelies would like to spend the night with your family?"

"You're our family!" Chiara said, shocked that he'd forgotten.

He kissed her head. "Yes, but you do need to make peace with your parents."

"But they're so—Mum is—" Chiara stopped abruptly. She'd remembered Yannick had never known his parents. Awkward as their relationship with Nina was, it was nothing to having two whole generations missing from your life, as Yannick had. She slipped her hand inside his shirt and braced it against his chest, feeling his heart beat steadily against her palm. "Yes, we will go to them, but not tonight. I need to be with you tonight," she whispered.

They were still standing in a three-way embrace when a tone sounded from out in the café.

Chiara glanced about. "Is that my phone?"

Lili said, "Can't be. We left them in the van."

The tone sounded again.

Then a phone rang.

"That might be *Tante*'s business number . . . someone wanting a table booking," Chiara said uneasily.

Lili lifted her head away from Yannick's shoulder. "Why isn't she answering it?"

"Probably still talking to Dequan."

"Yes, but—" The phone stopped.

Tone.

The phone began to ring again.

Chiara moved away reluctantly. "We'd better check that," she said to Yannick.

"And I'd better finish this batter."

The kitchen and the café were both empty, and Chiara looked about for inspiration. "*Tante*? Dequan?"

There was no answer. Martina's phone wasn't on any of the tables, and it wasn't near the till.

Staffroom?

She was still looking in there when the phone rang again.

This time, it kept on ringing, and she tracked it into the café, where Lili and Yannick were in the act of opening a hold-all.

Chiara stared at it for a moment and then said, "That's Dequan's."

Lili raised her voice. "Yes, but we can't just let it keep ringing. It might be important." She fished about and came up with a phone. Just as she held it out, the ringing stopped.

Ping.

Wordlessly, Lili held it out to Yannick.

He took it and held it to the light. "I think I can see the pattern on the screen . . ."

The phone rang again. Yannick ran his finger in a quick zigzag and the screen lit up.

"Answer it," Chiara mouthed.

"Hello? This is Dequan . . ." Yannick put his hand over the screen. "What's his other name?"

"Qin," Chiara said.

He raised a thumb.

"This is Dequan Qin's phone."

"Finally!" The voice pouring through the speaker sounded exasperated. "This is Takk. I've been trying to call you for hours."

Yannick shot a dismayed look at Chiara and Lili. "Now what?"

"I need you to come to the pick-up location right now, Mister Qin."

"I'm not Mister Qin," Yannick said hastily.

"Then—"

"My name is Yannick Langel."

"Are you saying I've been calling the wrong flaming number all this time?"

"If you want to talk to Mister Qin, you have the right

number. He's just not available."

There was an audible huff from the other end of the phone. "Give me strength! Will you please get Mister Qin to call me ASAP? My job's on the line, here."

Maybe this struck a chord with Yannick because he said, "Just a moment, Ms . . . Mister —"

The voice was young and husky, and it could have been either.

"Mistress, if you want to be formal. Mistress Takk Engel. Uh — Langel. You're alpenfee?"

"Yes. Why?"

"Never mind, I just thought the name was familiar. Master Langel, I need to execute this job. I'm hanging on by my toe-nails because my manner isn't exactly the poker-up sort they want at V-S. I flimflammed my way into it, and then I got the *very thin ice* speech from a hob man at the Victorian office. He's small but deadly. And now I've gone and smashed an-other cardinal rule and given you my last name. Do me a fa-vour and put it out of your mind. *Please* get Mister Qin for me."

The young woman sounded desperate.

"Wait. We'll see what we can do."

Yannick lifted his gaze to the twins. "This is your call, love-lies. I think Mistress Martina must have gone into her house, and it's not my place to go yelling for her in there."

"*Gott im Himmel!*" Lili sounded panicked. "What's she do-ing that she didn't hear all that noise and make Dequan an-swer his phone?"

"She's doing Dequan, that's what she's doing," Chiara said.

The phone quacked urgently. "Hanging by my toenails here, remember!"

Yannick said, "If she's with her man, she won't want *me* there. Lovelies, this one's something for you to sort out."

Chiara nodded and took the phone.

She reached for Lili's hand, and they went through into *Tante* Martina's cottage.

"I'll check the kitchen. You try the sitting room," she said to Lili.

Lili clung on. "No . . . together."

"Right . . ."

A quick tour of the ground floor and the little garden assured them *Tante* Martina wasn't entertaining her guest in any sedate and interruptible way.

The twins exchanged despairing looks and started up the spiral stair.

CHAPTER TWENTY: BEFORE THE WITCHING HOUR

Lili, December Thirty-first

Lili clung to Chiara's hand as they reached the small landing.

Tante Martina's bedroom door was closed.

Lili swallowed. "We *can't* do this."

The phone squawked.

"Shush!" Chiara said into the speaker.

She thrust the phone at Lili and tapped on the door.

Silence . . . and then a laughing gasp.

Lili felt the blood mounting in her cheeks. To stand here listening was worse than—

"*Tante?*"

Silence, and then a muffled gurgle. She pictured Yannick as he moaned against her breast or Chiara's mouth.

"*Tante?* Dequan?"

And then *Tante* Martina's voice exploded into anger. "*Gott im Himmel!* What the devil do you *want*?"

Lili pushed the door open gently. She felt Chiara's cheek pressed against hers as they peeped in. To her relief, *Tante* Martina was dressed. On the other hand, she was sitting on the bed with the spectacular Christmas coverlet she'd been sewing all year pulled up over her legs.

"Sorry, *Tante* Martina, but there's a call—" she said.

Chiara added, "It's for Dequan, and the person says it's urgent."

Their aunt's grey eyes flashed with fury. "I can't imagine anything was urgent enough for you to come interrupting us."

Us?

Lili said hastily, "I know. We've been awful, but we—"

"What about this call?" Martina sounded a little less furious. Her face was flushed, and she glanced betrayingly down towards her legs and pushed her hand under the cover.

"It's for Dequan," Chiara said.

Lili took a deep breath and then another. She was torn between hysteria and sympathy. It would be *awful* to be interrupted by—say, Tab or Josefa or—*Gott im Himmel!* Mum!—at such a moment. She said gently, "You can let him come up for air. I should think he's back to his brain by now."

She edged through the door and held out the phone.

Martina stared at it. "Where did you get that?"

She was about to explain when the coverlet heaved and humped, and Dequan Qin emerged. He, too, was dressed, but he looked ruffled and rumpled. His mouth was curled in an irresistible smile. He nodded to Lili. "Hello again, twin."

Lili gave him a great many points for composure.

Chiara said from behind her, "There's no need to be embarrassed, Dequan. I expect you don't want to talk right now, but this person—"

Tante Martina clicked her fingers. The phone flashed out of Lili's hand and she squeaked with shock as her fingers snapped shut on thin air.

Tante looked at the screen and sighed before holding the thing out to her lover. "I think this must be your phone. I'll leave you to deal with it while I deal with *them*."

To Lili's consternation, her aunt got out of bed and advanced on the door.

"Out."

The single word was enough to send Lili and Chiara scurrying down the stairs.

Martina herded them into the sitting room where, to Lili's enormous relief, Yannick was seated on the couch.

Martina, with red spots flaring on her cheeks, glowered at him. "Out. This is family business."

Yannick glared back at her. "I am family." He held out both arms, and Lili and Chiara fled to the warmth and safety of his embrace. He gave them a hug. "Okay, my lovelies?"

"Yes—" Lili gasped.

"*Tante* Martina's just—" Chiara went on.

"A bit—"

"Stop that." *Tante* pointed at Lili. Lili felt the tug of a compulsion.

Gott im Himmel! She pressed into Yannick's embrace.

Martina seemed to have worked herself into another cold rage. She went on pointing at Lili. "You. Tell me why you had Dequan's phone. You, Chiara, keep quiet. Yannick, go away."

Yannick made no move, except to tighten his grip.

Lili fought the compulsion and then gave up. "After you and Dequan went upstairs to yodel one another, we saw Dequan had left his bag. We kept hearing texts and messages pinging."

Chiara said, "And then—"

Martina's pointing finger oriented on Chiara. "Quiet." It moved to Yannick. "Out."

Lili clutched at his arm, but his steady breathing told her he wasn't going anywhere. She continued. "And then the phone rang. It kept on ringing and ringing and we thought it must be important."

"So—" Chiara tried to help out.

"Hush," *Tante* Martina said.

Lili felt their husband draw breath. He said, in a hard voice she'd never heard from him, "Hush yourself. Stop bullying my wives."

Tante Martina choked. "Your—*Gott im Himmel! Großer Gott im Himmel!* Nina is going to *kill* me!"

Yannick went on, "I answered the phone. The person

111

wanted to speak to Dequan Qin right now. She said it was urgent. That's why my lovelies brought the phone to you. We didn't think you'd want me in there."

Martina goggled at him, and Lili realised her aunt had possibly never heard him say so much before. He must have spoken during their initial interview, but that was years . . .

The door opened, and *Tante* Martina's smiling lover came in. He wasn't smiling now. He looked distressed.

Ignoring Lili, Chiara and Yannick, he held out his arms to *Tante* Martina.

She went into them.

Just the way we go to Yannick.

"What, *mein Liebe*?" *Tante* Martina's voice was gentle.

Her man held her with what looked like desperation. "It's the V-S driver. She's here. She's been messaging for three hours, but my phone was in the B&B, and it wasn't working."

What?

"What's V-S?" Lili mouthed. The woman on the phone had mentioned that.

Chiara leaned forward to see past Yannick and mouthed back, "I don't know."

Martina had gone still. "V-S already?"

Dequan said, "I forgot. I plain put it out of my mind. Martina . . . I tried to put her off, but she says she'll lose her job if I don't come now. She's contracted to return me to my pick-up point today."

Lili felt sick. There was so much pain in both their voices.

"Yannick —" She felt tears behind her eyes.

"I'll see what I can do." Yannick extricated himself from between her and Chiara and went out.

Tante Martina sobbed . . .

No . . .

Chiara started sniffling.

A loud honking sounded outside.

When it continued, the pair pulled apart, and Dequan

strode out.

Tante Martina turned blindly and sank onto the couch in the spot Yannick had vacated.

Lili put her arm around her aunt. Her heart hurt in sympathy.

"It's all right, *Tante*," Chiara murmured.

Lili couldn't speak, because she knew she'd start sobbing. It wasn't her place to be distressed. *She* had her husband, her twin, and a glorious life to enjoy. She put her cheek on *Tante* Martina's shoulder, but her aunt had gone into a peculiar state somewhere between slumped and rigid.

Soul-cold. The expressive term for fairy depression echoed in Lili's mind.

Nina said there was no such thing.

It can't have gone that far. On Boxing Day she hadn't even met him!

Chiara whispered, "We went from wishing to priested . . ."

"That's different. We've known Yannick for—"

"Years. I know, but—"

"Do you think—"

"She's wished?"

Tante Martina made no sign of hearing their hurried conversation.

The door opened again, and Yannick strode in. He took in the situation and snapped, "*Tante* Martina, get cracking."

Martina stirred at last. "What?"

Yannick said, "Move. I just spent my holiday bonus on a Vouch-Safe voucher for you and talked the driver into servicing it now instead of waiting for a vacancy. Go." He jerked his head.

She said, "The café—"

Lili felt the knot of trouble dissolving, unravelling, and uncomplicating as their husband once more scattered preconceptions. She gave *Tante* Martina a comforting hug. "We'll look after that."

"We'll look after everything," Chiara said.

Yannick sighed loudly. "Get going. There are six geese a laying out there honking the place down."

Martina went on sitting there, but she made a sudden move, and Lili saw she'd conjured a face cloth. She mopped her face.

Lili took it out of her hand and saw she'd found a napkin as well.

She must be really messed up to start conjuring Christmas napkins.

A black line on the napkin tugged at her memory.

Just Eloped . . .

She felt a hysterical giggle building up.

"Yannick?"

Yannick held out his hands, and Lili and Chiara got up, lifting their quivering aunt between them. Yannick managed to get his arms around all three.

"Come on, *Tante*," he said.

The horn outside was still honking.

"That driver won't wait forever . . ."

He conjured the door open and together, the three of them propelled Martina out to the waiting car.

For some reason, there were six geese and a number of eggs on the pavement. The geese, maybe stirred by the horn, were honking and shuffling and beating their wings, but as soon as Martina passed them, they fell silent.

Dequan stood beside the car, apparently arguing with the driver who had got out of the car with a tablet in her hand.

Lili gaped at the extraordinary figure who must be Takk Engel.

She had long fair hair, high-laced black boots and *wings*.

No. Lili blinked, and the shadowy wings were gone.

Dequan turned and spotted Martina. "Please, *fräulein*?" He held out his hand.

She went to him, and they vanished into the car.

114

Takk Engel snapped her gaze around to the three of them. "Finally!" She puffed out her cheeks. Her eyes, which were very blue, sharpened and she stared at them. "Um—no. You're not my problem. Crikey Daniel, I've got to go. Gotta get this pair back to Sydney and get them into a bed before the witching hour. Thanks for the help . . . you girls . . . you've got an A-grade gold-plated unraveller there. Mind you look after him."

She got into the car and drove away.

The geese shuffled into motion and set off down the street, parading in a neat line.

"WTF?" Lili said helplessly.

Chapter Twenty-one: Happy New Year

Yannick, January First

Midnight came and went in *Langelhame.*
Yannick was unaware of the exact moment that one year transitioned into the next, but it was breaking dawn when he remembered it was New Year's Day.

At that point, he was lying blissfully in the bed with his lovelies snuggled against him. They were hot and damp from exertion, and his ears still rang from their high-pitched joyful yodels.

He wondered if Mistress Martina's man felt as blissed out as he did.

One of his lovelies sat up.

"What's wrong, Lili?" he asked sleepily.

"I need chocolate."

He felt a stab of regret. "I'm sorry. I don't have any."

"Luckily, *we* do." Lili snapped her fingers, and he heard some rustles as she dealt with wrappers in the faint light.

She leaned over him and pushed a chocolate into his mouth. "Something nice for you to suck on. Not as nice as me, but it will do for now."

She rustled again and said, "Catch, Chi."

His fair-haired bride fought out of the covers and groped around for the chocolate she must have failed to intercept.

He wondered what else they'd brought through the gates in their bags.

"Lovelies, did you talk to your parents?"

Lili said, "No, but—"

"We sent a long letter—" Chiara finished.

"We told them that we love them —"

"And that we'll come to see them soon —"

"And we asked if Luca could come —"

"And stay with us sometimes when we're settled . . ."

"We said to let us know —"

"When they'd like to visit us at *Langelhame*."

Yannick sighed. He supposed that would do. His lovelies had to manage their own affairs. If their first family came to *Langelhame,* he would make them welcome.

Lili said, "What's V-S?"

"It's a company that arranges vouchers for mystery holidays. Drivers take people who buy them or are given them to their destination and then come to bring them home. Takk told me while I was arranging Mistress Martina's voucher."

"Oh." Lili rustled some more wrappers and lobbed more chocolates at him and Chiara.

"What about the geese?" She sounded as if she was talking through a mouthful.

"I don't know. Probably part of a Christmas wish that went off at a tangent."

"Like our apples," Lili said.

"Which you *totally* stole."

Yannick laughed. His lovelies would never let him forget that piece of opportunistic larceny. He stretched, and he kissed a stray shoulder.

A gentle hand stroked back his hair, possibly leaving a smear of chocolate in its wake.

A whole day off to spend with my lovelies.

"Three o'clock start tomorrow," he said.

Chiara said, "What?"

"I have to get the baking done. We promised to look after the café until *Tante* Martina gets back."

"I hope she brings Dequan with her when she comes," Lili said.

"It will be awkward if she doesn't."

"I'm sure they'd manage something," Yannick said.

"Why are you sure?"

"I'm sure because *we* would manage something. And what we manage tomorrow is a three o'clock baking start."

"What if we lovelies don't want to get up at two every morning?" Chiara asked.

"Bicycles," Yannick said.

"What?"

"You have bicycles. We'll leave your bicycles at Grene's Motor Clinic along with the van each night. I'll drive the van to the café as usual, and you lovelies can ride in when you're ready."

"What if it's raining?" Chiara objected.

"Or snowing . . ." Lili demurred.

"Or if we feel tired after our wifely duties—"

"Which wifely duties?"

Chiara jack-knifed on the bed and kissed his belly.

Lili hitched his shoulders so he rested cheek to cheek with her breasts.

"These," they said in chorus.

"Look, lovelies!" Yannick said, and he pointed to the sky-light, where three black swans sailed serenely over Nordalp, winging their way back home.

ABOUT THE AUTHOR

Lark Westerly lives on the island state of Tasmania.

One of her favourite occupations is weaving stories about the mix of fairy and human characters in the *Fairy in the Bed, Red Cat* and *Pixie Grip* series.

To find out more about the *Fairy in the Bed* world, visit Lark virtually at https://larksinger.weebly.com